Angshu Dasgupta lives in Kolkata with his spouse and two daughters. He is a computer programmer by profession. This is his first work of fiction.

'Angshu Dasgupta has achieved a beautiful balance...We learn of the awful pain inflicted on Orko, the adolescent at the heart of this book, by both others and himself. Despite this sad undertone, the text has a surprising lightness about it...even when Orko is at his most wretched, there is a glimmer of hope carried by a thread of resilience...Dasgupta has written a novel of fortitude and ultimately peace, clarity and braveness.'

—*IndianLink News*

'A coming-of-age novel about [a young boy], Orko, as he tries to map out the world through his experiences and to make sense of his life and identity. Dasgupta deftly conjures up the essence of 1980s' Calcutta [where] Orko grows up, relating to everything "feminine". The narrative effortlessly deals with the questions of gender roles and behaviour, peer pressure, religion, class, as well as the nature of truth and reality. What is more, the author achieves this by saying very little and relying more on the observations of his protagonist...[A] promising debut in fiction.'

—*The Telegraph*

'[*Fern Road Boy*] will not only resonate with those who are young and confused but also remind adults what it is to be a child, discovering one's own identity in a country where everything dangerously treads the line of becoming taboo...[A] memorable read.'

—*purplepencilproject.com*

FERN ROAD BOY

Angshu Dasgupta

SPEAKING
TIGER

SPEAKING TIGER BOOKS LLP
125-A, Ground Floor, Shahpur Jat
New Delhi – 110049

First published in Australia by UWAP, University of Western Australia, and in India by Speaking Tiger Books, 2019

This edition published by Speaking Tiger Books, 2021

ISBN: 978-93-5447-207-7

10 9 8 7 6 5 4 3 2 1

Printed at Chaman Enterprises, New Delhi

For Aardvark

One

Fern Road is not a road lined with ferns. It is a labyrinthine lane, lined with practical, sturdy houses, two and three storeys high. Their windows have wooden shutters, with columns of slats that open and shut like giant mechanical eyelids. The houses look like they've been here forever, their balconies floating above the narrow footpaths like magic carpets.

Orko hurries through the maze, turning left, right, right again, then left. In the corner is a two-storey house, its bright green gate framed by purple bougainvillea. In the mornings, an old man reads his newspaper on the verandah, a cup of tea on a teapoy by his side. In the afternoon, the man stands by the railing, smiling at strangers as they walk past. There's no one on the verandah today – just pyjamas, a towel, a girl's school uniform and women's petticoats hung out to dry on a blue clothesline.

Around the corner are little shops that sell stationery, samosas, mutton; their minders doze behind weathered counters, on stools and in aluminium chairs. Orko walks past the shops, emerging at Golpark, which is not really a park – it's a little garden at a traffic roundabout, with an iron fence around it. There's a sweet shop at the corner of the roundabout. Orko casts about for loose change in his pockets; he's hungry.

A roshogolla, unlike the parks and roads with their delusions of grandeur, is exactly what it claims to be: a little ball of a sweetmeat swimming in a puddle of sugar syrup. Orko gulps it down, leaving the stainless-steel bowl in the sink.

He marks time at the bus stop, glancing at watches strapped on other people's wrists. Petite, with a delicate chain for a strap. Large and chunky, with a black dial. Digital, with a plastic band. After ten minutes or so, the bus he's waiting for trundles along. He takes the only vacant seat, next to a tired-looking young man with a sling bag across his shoulder.

They leave Golpark behind and ascend the Dhakuria bridge. To the left is the Children's Little Theatre; Orko has been there a few times, with his grandmother. From the crest of the bridge, he can see the railway tracks below. A green suburban train sidles along, its horn booming over the noisy traffic. A startled calf hastily moves out of its path. The gears grind as the asthmatic bus nears the foot of the bridge, the dull whine of its engine giving way to a gentle growl. On either side of the street are shopfronts and residential apartments. Five schoolgirls wait patiently at a pedestrian crossing. An auto-rickshaw slows down near them. One of the girls shakes her head, and the auto-rickshaw picks up speed again.

The bus come to a halt near a crowded intersection. The driver kills the engine. When the lights change to green, the engine doesn't start on the first try. Just as they're about to cross the intersection, the lights change again. The brakes let out a mournful howl as they lurch to a stop.

After the intersection, the footpaths are narrower, skirting high walls punctuated by large iron gates. Some of the gates have arches, marked with uninteresting text in raised metal lettering. Beyond the gates are tall, forlorn buildings, fronted by unkempt lawns and derelict carports. When they're about to reach the university, the young man beside Orko leaves his seat. He rings the bell and makes his way to the door, just as the bus is slowing to a halt. The conductor demands to see his ticket, but the man hops off without a word.

The bus continues, making slow progress amid a sea of bicycles, rickshaws and pedestrians. Orko is alert now, looking out for the bend in the road after which he must disembark. He reaches for the handrail as the bus crawls around the bend. He holds out his ticket for the conductor, who waves him on. He crosses the street and makes his way to the mouth of a lane that bleeds off to the right of the thoroughfare.

The lane is dark and narrow. It winds between high walls plastered with election propaganda in raucous red. It snakes to the right; the walls fall away. To the left is a vacant plot, with a makeshift fence around it. To the right is a rusty green gate, ajar, the latch broken.

Beside the gate is a dilapidated metal signboard on a rusty stalk. 'Bidyasagar Kanan,' it says, in English and in Bangla. At its foot, faded lettering on a slab of marble declares that this residential enclave was inaugurated by the Honourable Minister for Education in January 1973. A narrow concrete driveway leads into the enclave. To its left is a deserted guardhouse; to its right is a parking lot – a rusty old Ambassador, the colour of a withering plantain leaf, its only occupant.

The car hasn't been driven in Orko's lifetime. It looks like it has sprung from the earth – the result, perhaps, of a wayward spell cast by an itinerant conjurer. Its tyres are flat, with tufts of grass growing around them. The round headlights and the chrome grille, curving earthward at the extremities, give it a permanent, forbidding frown. A giant gulmohur tree overlooks the parking lot; crows congregate among its branches, pelting the car with excrement as they wing their way to and from their perch. As a young child, Orko would often climb into the car and sit in the driver's seat, his legs dangling a few inches above the floor. He would put the car in gear and pretend to drive off. Sometimes he would drive himself to Dehradun; sometimes he would just drive to Gariahat market to buy a fat pig.

The enclave consists of eight identical buildings, with a tangled web of cobbled paths snaking around them. The buildings, each four storeys high, look like a child built them from a box of Lego on a slow afternoon. Orko lives in one of these buildings – the one closest to the parking lot, beside the gulmohur. There are two bicycles parked beneath the stairs. The red one belongs to Orko; his father bought it for him on his thirteenth birthday. He climbs the dark staircase, counting out forty-two steps. A few strides to the left brings him to the front door of his flat.

The nameplate on the letterbox simply reads 'Dr Nandan Sengupta, PhD'. Orko shrugs off his schoolbag and fishes a keyring out of his pocket. The room inside is shaped like an L, with a wooden sofa set occupying the short leg. At the end of the other is a round dining table with three mismatched chairs. The refrigerator is by the dining table, beside the door to his bedroom.

On the refrigerator, in a wooden photo frame, is the picture of a young woman in a saree, sitting on a park bench. It is one of two photographs Orko has of his mother. There is a wedding photo on his father's desk, but Nandan keeps it face-down, under a stack of papers and periodicals. Orko looks at it sometimes, and it never fails to startle him. Nandan is clean-shaven in the picture; he is wearing a dark suit, and looks mildly amused. Orko's mother is in a saree that could be red, or mauve – it's impossible to tell from the black-and-white photograph. She looks frightening, with the nose pin and the oversized earrings. They're seated about six inches from one another; they could be strangers, posing for a photograph to commemorate a chance encounter.

In Orko's room, a simple narrow bed is positioned directly beneath the ceiling fan. Along the far wall is an ancient writing desk that had belonged to his grandfather. There's a clothes horse to the right, and a pair of box windows to the left. Below the window ledge are four shelves full of cassettes. He counts the cassettes every now and then; at last count, there were four hundred and sixty-three. On the top shelf is an old stereo – a hand-me-down from an uncle. Three of the four walls are completely unadorned. On the wall that stretches from the door to the wardrobe is a poster of Tracy Chapman. To her right is Jack Nicholson, as the Joker. On the door of the wardrobe is a reproduction of the cover of a Guns N' Roses album, *Use Your Illusion*, in electric blue. Orko doesn't particularly like the band anymore, but he can't rip off the poster – he used too much glue when he put it up.

There is just one bathroom in the flat. The shower head is caked with lime and rust. It's a test of patience trying to get anything from it. Orko fills the metal bucket from the tap and hastily pours mugs of tepid water on his head. He doesn't bother with soap – he's hungry.

In the refrigerator are stacks of bowls covered with melamine plates, and the thought of sorting through them makes him wish he was having lunch at Urmi's. Urmi is in Orko's class, and up until a few months ago the two of them rode the school bus home every afternoon. They would run up the stairs to her first-floor flat. 'We're hungry,' Urmi would announce as soon as her mother ('Ketaki-mashi' to Orko) opened the door.

Lunch at Urmi's was a grand affair – a minimum of three courses. When he was sure he could eat no more, Ketaki-mashi would insist that he hadn't eaten at all; he must have another serving of fish, another helping of dessert.

Soon after Orko turned fifteen, his father said it was time he stopped using the school bus.

'How will I go to school, then?' Orko asked.

'Well, it's easy enough to take the public bus,' Nandan said. 'There are many that'll take you very close to your school. I'll show you tomorrow.'

'But all my friends take the school bus,' Orko protested.

'You can't really know the city and the people that live in it if you don't share in the daily ritual of using public transport,' Nandan said.

Orko couldn't respond to a sentence as complicated as that. He suspected that his father knew this, and that the sentence had been framed long ago, in anticipation of a conversation in which it might come of use.

The next morning, they took the bus to Golpark. His father led him through Fern Road – a right turn, a left, another left, then right again, Orko carefully noted. They went past Gariahat market and across the tramline, into a lane that looked like it was a dead end. They passed through a passageway between two houses – a gnarly old house to the right, a newer house with pink walls to the left. The passage was so narrow that they had to walk in single file. When they emerged, Orko was surprised to find himself on the route the school bus took every morning.

'Does this look familiar?' his father asked.

Orko nodded.

Nandan left him there, with a letter for the school administrator, asking that he be allowed to leave by himself at the end of the day. Orko followed the footpath faithfully. Cars and buses overtook him. Someone waved at him through the rear window of a passing school bus. Orko was too startled to wave back.

At the end of the day, he went to the office with the letter from his father. Mrs Bannerjee, the administrator, read the letter carefully. She looked at Orko over the top of her eyeglasses.

'So you're all grown up now, are you?' she said, with a smile. She wrote out a gate pass and handed it to Orko.

'Look right and then left when you cross the street,' she said.

Orko smiled. He had been crossing busy streets by himself since he was ten.

'I will, miss,' he said.

The next morning, Nandan handed him the bus fare, and 'a little extra, just in case'. Orko was on his own.

For the first few days, it was a bit of a bother, especially on the way back. He had to show his pass to the guard at the school gates. He lost his way a few times when he was heading to Golpark. Sometimes all the seats on the bus were taken, and he wished he was in the school bus with Urmi, in the seat they always shared, three rows from the back.

Now Orko likes walking out of school, to Gariahat and down the boulevard. Sometimes he dawdles, browsing through the racks of magazines and second-hand books in the little stalls. Sometimes he stops at the music shop at the end of the boulevard, blowing all his pocket money on pirated cassettes. When he's hungry, like he was today, he takes the shortcut through Fern Road and buys himself a snack from one of the shops at the roundabout.

He doesn't have lunch with Urmi anymore, because he reaches home a good half-hour after the school bus. Lunch is in the fridge, in the stack of bowls covered with melamine plates. Nandan has taught him to make rice. He makes exactly as much as he wants, and because the rice is steaming hot he doesn't have to heat the vegetables or the dal.

He carries his lunch to his room. He sets the plate down on the window ledge and browses through his cassettes. After a few false starts, he settles on the greatest hits of Simon & Garfunkel. He turns up the volume before hoisting himself into the box window.

Outside, the afternoon is still, the sky an unforgiving blue, with not a cloud in sight. There's not a quiver in the leaves on the trees – it's as if they're frozen in place. Down below, a clutch of buildings crowd around a little playground, its border marked out by a cement footpath. Rusty swing sets, a slide, a seesaw, a sandpit without any sand in it – it looks like the abandoned work of a distracted artist, the footpath its sorry frame.

Every family living in these buildings has some connection with the university. Orko's father is a professor in the department of electrical engineering. Urmi's father, Dr Datta, is an administrator. No one has moved in or out of the enclave in Orko's lifetime.

Their flat is among a handful that have a telephone. Every once in a while, the phone rings. When it's for Mrs Sen, Orko fetches her from the adjoining flat. When it's for someone living further away, he transforms into a teletype machine. It's almost as if the message flows directly from his ear to his fingertips, without passing the gates of his comprehension. He carefully inscribes the name and the flat number of the intended recipient on the top left corner of the note. When he's done, it looks much like a telegram – staccato sentences, missing parts of speech – conveying a message that's of no interest to him. He folds it in half and runs across to deliver it.

'It's really difficult to get a phone connection,' Nandan told Orko when their telephone was installed a few months ago. 'Sometimes one forgets that one lives in a civilised country. Until everyone has a phone, those of us who do have a responsibility towards everybody else. After all, we didn't pay for the cable to be brought to our door. The government did.'

Orko's services seldom go unrewarded. The first slice of a cake, fresh out of the oven; a bowl of homemade potato wafers; a jam sandwich made of thin arrowroot biscuits. Orko never declines.

In the kitchen, by the stove, are eight glass jars of varying sizes. The largest jar is half-full of rice. By its side are two smaller jars, filled with different varieties of dal. The smallest jars contain spices – turmeric, bay leaves, cumin seeds, chilli powder, black pepper. The jars are covered in a coat of grime. In the corner, by the sink, is an ashtray overflowing with orange cigarette butts. In the sink, near the maker's mark, is a fissure, its spidery legs reaching out, upwards, downwards, sideways. Over the sink is a window, its grille coated with rust and grime.

Orko remembers sitting on the kitchen floor with his mother, the glass jars in a huddle between them. They wiped down the jars with dishrags soaked in soapy water. His mother taught him to blow bubbles, through a tiny hoop fashioned out of a length of insulated electrical wire. They would sit there, in the sweltering heat, blowing bubbles, eating mangoes, the sparkling jars back on the kitchen shelf.

Once, Orko threw a mango seed out of the window. His mother admonished him: 'What if it hits someone on the head?' She made him go downstairs and bring the seed back. They gave it a burial in the large tub of compost she kept on the balcony by the kitchen.

In this kitchen of his memories, the walls are a brilliant white. The jars twinkle; their contents glow yellow, and orange, and sparkling white, like dabs of paint on a still-life watercolour. The window grille is so white it hurts the eye. He isn't tall enough to see Urmi's flat through the window, although he can see the terrace of the building in which she lives. Above the terrace is the vast blue expanse where he first saw a vulture.

'Look!' his mother said, kneeling beside him, pointing through the window. At the tip of her finger, against the bright blue sky, was a large black bird.

'A crow!'

'Is that what it is?' The fingertip was gone now, and Orko followed the shape as it spiralled downwards, in slow, ever-tightening circles, its wings barely moving. When it banked, Orko knew that it couldn't possibly be a crow.

'An eagle?' That was the only large bird that he could think of.

'It's a vulture,' his mother said.

Today, the sky is without blemish. Underneath is a patch of earth, with splashes of grass left behind by the monsoon. A badminton net, strung between two metal posts of indeterminate colour. Urmi's balcony. Urmi's school tunic, drying on the clothesline.

Urmi is in Orko's earliest memories. When they were very young, their mothers met every morning in Urmi's flat. The children played in Urmi's room while their mothers shared a pot of tea in the kitchen. Sometimes his mother would leave him there while she ran errands. They shared Orko's books and Urmi's toys. They learned to ride a bicycle at about the same time; they would tear around the enclave, much to the consternation of the old caretaker. They played in the old car in the parking lot, pretending they were going on an expedition to the Himalayas. At school they were classmates from the beginning. Sometimes their teachers wouldn't let them sit side by side, because they talked too much. In the lunch break they would climb the tree in the schoolyard and sit astride their favourite bough, eating unripe guavas and laughing about things that Orko can no longer remember.

In the winter, they spent every Saturday afternoon on Urmi's terrace. They brought puffed rice with them, and a stack of Enid Blyton's books. They sat there on the terrace, the bowl of puffed rice between them, embroiled in separate adventures with a boy detective called Frederick Algernon Trotteville (Fatty to his friends). Fatty was brave. He was brilliant. He was cheeky. They both adored him, and they fought over him.

'He's my best friend!'

'No, he's mine!'

'Prove it!'

'I'll give him all my toys.'

'He won't like your toys. He's a boy. Then we'll see who he likes better.'

'Then I won't let you play with my toys.'

That shut Orko up, because he hated his toys – a handful of dinky cars, a golliwog, a panda, a stack of jigsaw puzzles, a replica of Big Ben. Urmi's room, on the other hand, was a wonderland. There were dolls everywhere – princess dolls, a grandma doll, a baby that cried if you pulled the pacifier out of its mouth, and a little girl doll with her own bicycle. Every time Orko thought he had seen all of Urmi's dolls, a new one would emerge from under the bed, or from the top shelf of her cupboard. There was a doll's house whose roof came off, so they could rearrange the furniture. There was a kitchen set, with a gas stove, a pressure cooker, an array of pots and pans, and a dinner service. There was a tea set – a tiny teapot, with matching cups and saucers, a milk jug, and a tray, made of plaster, laden with biscuits and scones. When they tired of the dolls, they would turn the study table into Toadstool House. He had to be Noddy. She always got to be Big Ears, with his magic spells.

At the time, Urmi was a little bigger than Orko, and often he would wear one of her frocks over his own clothes. Sometimes they were princesses, and they had just run away from an ogre who had kidnapped them from their father's castle. Sometimes they were fairies, jealously guarding the idyll of their village. Sometimes they were just themselves – Urmi and Orko, playing snakes and ladders. He couldn't give up all of that because of a silly fight over a boy in a book.

'We can share him, can't we?' he asked, in conciliatory tone.

'Hmph,' said Urmi, as she turned a page.

That was when the crow appeared. When he landed, his wings were in a tangle; they flapped about messily as he teetered on the edge of the parapet around the terrace. After he had gathered himself, though, he was the very embodiment of grace. He pranced and he preened, picking out bits of detritus lodged in his feathers. His lustrous beak shone in the afternoon sun. They named him Fatty, after their hero. He was cocky. He was fearless. He was beautiful.

They didn't know where Fatty lived, only that he knew they would be on the terrace every Saturday with treats for him. They loved the way Fatty cocked his head, a little leery at first of the feast laid out for him by the inscrutable humans. He would then peck away daintily at the puffed rice. When it had all disappeared, he would cock his head again to see if they had anything more for him. He would strut about, cawing at them, before flying away to his perch in the giant gulmohur tree by the parking lot.

Fatty kept them company through that winter. He seemed to know when to come looking for them.

'Do you think he can count to seven?' Orko asked Urmi one day, after Fatty flew away.

'Don't be silly. Crows can't count.'

'How does he remember to come every Saturday, then?' he countered.

'Well, I don't know,' said Urmi.

'What if he comes every day?'

One Saturday, when Fatty failed to appear, they decided he had gone to France with his parents. They waited eagerly for him to return, but he never did.

The last time Orko went to Urmi's flat was a few weeks ago. He was at her front door, and just as he was about to ring the bell, he heard Urmi's voice.

'That ungrateful brat,' she said. 'I never want to see him again.'

'You mustn't be cruel to him,' her mother said. 'His mother is gone, and his father chooses to live here, instead of moving in with his parents. Please, be nice to him.'

Orko shrank away from the doorbell. He tiptoed down the stairs and ran back home.

That morning, Urmi had announced to her friends that she was moving to a different school after their board exams. It was an elite girls' school, and Orko's mother was an alumna. Orko was jealous; it wasn't fair – why did Urmi get to go to his mother's school? How could she brag about it, knowing that he couldn't follow her there?

'You're such a show-off,' he said to her. They didn't speak for the rest of the day.

Although Urmi is his best friend, Orko has always been jealous of her. It started when they were six years old, maybe seven. There was a dance recital at their school, and Urmi was one of the dancers. Orko wanted to be in the dance, but their class teacher told him he couldn't. The dance was only for the girls. She encouraged him to try out for the play the boys were putting on. Orko pleaded, cajoled and threw tantrums until his teacher relented.

On the day of the recital, the dancers were dressed in white sarees with red borders. They had flowers in their hair, the leaves and tendrils painted onto their foreheads in sandalwood paste. They pranced, they twirled, their bodies moving to the rhythm of the music. Orko was dressed in a green shirt and a pair of brown corduroy trousers that didn't fit, because they were borrowed for the occasion from an older cousin. His part was to stand, with his arms apart, and hold as still as possible. He was a tree, flowerless, devoid of life. After the dance, the boys in his class named him 'Palm Tree', after Tagore's poem of that name. They called him that all the time. He had to beg them to stop. Urmi didn't partake in the teasing, and Orko was grateful.

Now, Orko can't help but wonder if Urmi refrained from teasing him because her mother had asked her to be kind to him. He didn't need her kindness. He is glad they live here, in the enclave. He can't bear the thought of moving in with his father's family.

Orko's paternal grandparents live in a large house with a lawn in the front and a vegetable garden in the back. His grandmother and grandfather live on the ground floor, in separate rooms. His uncle, his aunt and their two children live on the first floor – Robi is two years older than Orko, Ria a month younger.

When he was younger, Orko and his parents went to the house every Sunday. The family ate lunch together. Orko's grandfather sat at the head of the table, flanked by his two sons. The children sat at the other end. Robi sat facing his grandfather, with Ria to his right. Orko sat opposite Ria. Two chairs remained vacant.

They always sat this way. Orko's mother and his aunt served everyone individually, while his grandmother supervised the kitchen staff.

There was no conversation during meals. 'Charm, chew, masticate and swallow,' his grandfather would say. They would start their meal only after Orko's grandfather had brought the first morsel of rice to his lips. The bitter gourd, and the dal, followed by a vegetable, followed by fish. It never changed. Nothing ever changed in that house.

When they finished, a servant cleared away the used plates and set three places, for Orko's grandmother, his mother and his aunt. Sometimes Orko and Ria lingered. Maybe they would get a handful of potato fritters, or overhear conversation about their new cousin, just born, in a foreign country, seven oceans away. Maybe they would learn that a wedding was to take place, or that their cook was going to be a grandmother, yet again. Sometimes the women let them stay, but on most afternoons they were shooed away.

After lunch, they had to be very quiet. The grown-ups retired to their rooms for a siesta. Orko's father still had a room in the house. The room was sparsely furnished, with a queen-sized bed, a writing desk and an armchair. Buried in Orko's memories is a faded picture of his mother, sleeping on that bed. He can't be sure how old he is in the picture. He can't remember if they spent the night, or if his mother was taking a siesta like the rest of the grown-ups.

Orko's father isn't in that picture. Perhaps he was in the living room, reading. Once, when he was about seven or eight (he can't remember if it was before or after his mother's passing), Orko had followed his father into the living room after they had finished lunch. Nandan settled into his favourite armchair, with a book he had picked out from one of the many bookshelves in the room. Orko sat in the chair that was beside his father's. He remembers that he was very quiet, and he didn't move or fidget. His father looked distinctly uncomfortable, his brow furrowed. He flipped through the pages of the book for a while. Then he shut it and placed it in his lap. 'Why don't you go and play with Ria?' he asked. Orko ran out of the room and up the stairs. He remembers looking for Ria, and not finding her. There were four bedrooms on the first floor, and all the doors were shut.

Orko wanted to run away, but to do that he would have to go past his father in the living room. It was summer; the terrace was out of bounds. So he did the next thing that came to mind. He shut himself in the bathroom.

It was a large bathroom, one of two on the first floor. It was the bathroom with the red mosaic floor. The mirror was set too high on the wall, so he turned a bucket upside down and stood on it. He switched on the shaving light. His face shone yellow.

By the mirror was a cabinet, and that was his first time opening it. Inside, among shaving paraphernalia and packets of hair colour, was a stick of eyeliner. He took the black pencil and drew little studs onto his earlobes. He parted his hair in the middle. It was an improvement, but he still wasn't happy. His hair was too short.

There was a tube of toothpaste on the ledge by the washbasin. He wanted to squeeze all of it out into a squiggly snake on the floor. He didn't, because he had done that once, and his mother had made him clean it up, all by himself. He squeezed out a drop on his finger and licked it with the tip of his tongue. It tasted horrible. He rinsed out his mouth, then ran out of the bathroom to look for Ria again.

In the winter, Ria and Orko spent these afternoons playing hopscotch on the terrace. In the summer, they were at loose ends – they played made-up games, or told each other stories about princesses and dragons. That afternoon Ria was nowhere to be found. Unlike her older brother, she didn't have a room to herself; she shared her parents' bedroom. Perhaps she was asleep with her parents.

Orko pretended that it was the dead of night, and that he had broken in. He tiptoed about the first floor, looking for treasure that he might plunder, but he was so bored that he decided to make his escape via the terrace. He ran up the stairs, only to find the door locked. He sat there, by the unyielding door, and tried to think of ways to make his father stop hating him.

When he came back down the stairs, his aunt was by the bathroom door. Orko's heart skipped a beat. He had left the light on, and the tube of toothpaste was still on the floor.

'I love your earrings,' his aunt said, smiling at him as she switched off the light.

Orko sometimes wished Ria lived with him and his father, in their flat. Try as he might, he can't imagine living in that big house with all those people and their laundry list of rules and regulations. He would rather eat with the women, but in that house no one ever asked children what they wanted to do. When Orko went there with his father, Nandan turned into a completely different man; Orko struggled to reconcile this stranger with the father who lived with him and cared for him.

If Urmi's mother knew all of this, she certainly wouldn't think that Orko would be better off in his grandfather's house. He bristles with indignation, because he doesn't want concessions just because he has no mother. He does not want to be fed to the gills, and he does not care to be friends with someone who is being kind to him just because her mother said she should.

Orko is at the Kalighat crematorium today, with his father, his uncle, his grandfather and a handful of other men, most of whom he has only met occasionally. There's conversation, about politics and about the partition of Bengal. He could believe that they were at a wedding reception, if it wasn't for the body of Jatin-dadu, his great-uncle, laid out on the rough-hewn bier a few feet away.

They've been waiting here for almost an hour now, on these concrete benches just outside the cremation hall. There's the distinctive crematorium smell in the air; after his first visit, Orko wrote about this smell in one of his notebooks, calling it the smell of death. Now, he thinks it was lazy shorthand for a complex bouquet of odours – there's the smell from the ovens, of course, but there's also the smell of burning incense, of tuberose and, strangely enough, of spoiling food. It isn't the smell of death, because the deaths that have brought the mourners here have occurred many hours ago.

Orko doesn't want to be here. His cousins aren't here. Robi is exempt on account of his ongoing school board examinations, Ria because she is a girl.

'He was your grandfather's oldest brother,' Nandan said when Orko tried to talk his way out of coming. 'You're supposed to show up when a family member dies. How would you feel if you had to bring my body to the crematorium all by yourself?'

Orko's aunt Sudeshna, his mother's sister, once told him that he had been too young to have gone to the crematorium with his mother's body. She insisted that he was in the room when they finally took his mother away. Orko has no memory of this. He tries to picture his mother's hearse, making its way to Kalighat. The mobile greenhouse carrying the body leads the procession. The family follows in white Ambassadors, scattering marigold petals and puffed rice to mark the path of the final journey. Just as the body is unloaded from the carriage and lined up for cremation, the scene fades away and he finds himself face to face with Jatin-dadu's body.

He can't imagine his mother's body, her nostrils and ear canals closed off with cottonwool, surrounded by callous, unfeeling men who are waiting impatiently to cast her into the oven. He closes his eyes; the voices fade away; images swirl, dreamlike, half-real, blue. He's six years old. They're swimming, Orko and his mother, in the ocean, where no one will find them.

'I never want to go to the crematorium again,' Orko declares at breakfast the next morning. None of his friends have ever been to the crematorium. Very few have even seen a dead body. His father responds with an aphorism about life and death and escapism, but Orko isn't really listening.

'We're all going to die,' his father continues. 'You must try not to be horrified by the process.'

Orko pictures a grown-up version of himself, sitting on the concrete bench at the crematorium. He is with yet another dead body. His manner is laconic, and he's completely at ease with the atmosphere of death around him. He participates actively in stultifying conversation with his kinsmen. He shakes his head, but the image refuses to fade.

'What is it?' his father asks.

'Nothing,' Orko replies.

He remembers visiting Jatin-dadu with his parents, many years ago.

'What do you want to be when you grow up?' the old man had asked him.

'I want to be like ma,' Orko replied, stealing a glance at his mother, seated across the room. It took some prodding from his father before he understood that he was being asked an entirely different question.

'I want to drive a train,' he said eventually.

Jatin-dadu let out a guffaw. 'You're very young. You'll figure something out when you're older. You could be an engineer, like your father. You could even be a doctor. The possibilities are endless.'

Orko didn't want to be like his father. He didn't want to go to the university every morning, with a steel tiffin box and a battered leather briefcase, wearing dark trousers and a full-sleeved shirt, white, with stripes so fine you couldn't see them from a few feet away. He wanted to drive his train with the wind, through tunnels and paddy fields and forests and along the seashore, for days on end, drinking from a bottle of Thums Up, lunching on sandwiches (cheese and tomato, like his mother made).

He knows now that he isn't going to be a train driver, and he isn't going to be like his mother. He still doesn't want to be like his father. He wants to fly, like a bird. He wants to learn how to play the guitar. He wants to dance, alone, beneath a starlit sky. Most of all, he wants to swim.

Orko's earliest memory is of drowning, almost. He remembers the shock from the cold water as it gave way to his flailing body. He gasped and he spluttered as the water closed in around him, gurgling in his ears. When his toes made contact with the floor, there was a deafening silence. He couldn't see anything for the bright blue all around him. He knew, instinctively, that no one could see him – he was all alone, at the bottom of the pool. He began to scream, but the water rushed into his lungs, and he thought that he was going to die.

Those terrifying moments are benign now, frozen in a series of still images, black, white and blue. His mother's hands in his armpits, the sweet sensation of air rushing into his lungs, treading water, forgetting to and sinking again, his mother's voice, an incantation in a forgotten language.

The memories are still available for immediate recall. He can smell the chlorine, and imagine the texture of his shrivelled fingertips. He remembers his mother's voice, coaxing him out of the water with the promise of ice cream. She held him, telling him he'd been very good, and that one day he was going to be a great swimmer. The smell of lavender talc fought the caustic odour of chlorine as she ushered him into the ladies' changing rooms. Afterwards, she took him to the ice cream booth and bought him a strawberry ice cream, in a waffle cone. They walked out of the club and boarded a tram. His mother fished out her coin purse from her large shoulder bag and counted out change for their tickets. The conductor declined to issue a ticket for Orko, telling his mother that her baby didn't need one. Orko remembers saying that he was not a baby – he was occupying a whole seat, and he knew how to swim.

There was a phase when he could stay afloat, and he could propel himself forward, but his arms and his legs moved as if they belonged to four different people. He would watch his mother wistfully as her lithe form scythed through the water with infinite grace. He wanted to be like her, in the water and out of it. He can't remember if it was that year or the next when he was finally able to keep up with her.

They went swimming every weekday, a few hours after lunch. Orko would pretend he was a baby whale swimming alongside his mother. He would follow her as she swam up and down the length of the pool. Sometimes he would peel off and swim on his own, for he was now the grown-up, and his babies wanted to play. So they swam together, by themselves. Underwater. Across lanes. Diagonally. In no particular direction at all. They would continue to swim, Orko and his pod, till his eyes burned from the chlorine and his fingertips shrivelled up like forgotten grapes. In the end, his mother would drag him from the pool and into the changing rooms, with its panels of varnished wood topped by a line of frosted glass that glistened with condensation.

They showered in neighbouring stalls. His mother hummed in the shower, and sometimes, when Orko recognised the tune, he would hum under his breath. They usually emerged together, because Orko turned off the shower when he heard his mother do the same across the panel that separated them. She had a towel on her head and another around her torso; Orko had just the one towel. She whisked him away to a cubicle and wiped him dry. He dressed himself, and she combed his hair. Then, he ran to the swing set in the playground.

On the swings, he learned that he couldn't move forward without going backwards first. He soared, like a kite, then swooped down. Soar again. Swoop. He was a bird with no name. He had a bright orange beak, and his feathers were a brilliant white. He longed to break free and fly away. He was always a little disappointed when he saw his mother as he soared in the air, her large jute bag slung over her shoulder. He liked it when she wore pants, because he wore pants too. They usually ate ice cream. Orko liked strawberry, his mother – butterscotch. They walked down the driveway, a stream of cars coming at them, windows rolled up. A few blasted their startled horns at them; the rest just drove past as if they were invisible.

The last time Orko went swimming, they got off the tram and walked into the club, like they always did. They walked along the driveway, hand in hand, Orko to his mother's left, away from the cars that whizzed past them. Just as they were about to go into the changing rooms, Orko felt a hand on his shoulder.

'I'm afraid he can't go in there,' said a voice. It was a woman's voice – stern, like his Bangla teacher's.

'But he always comes in with me,' said his mother. 'He's only seven!'

'I don't know about that – I can't let him into the ladies' changing rooms. He needs to go down there,' said the woman, pointing down the hallway. 'Around the corner.'

Orko was sure that it was a misunderstanding and that his mother would clear it up, but she fished out his swimming trunks from her bag and walked him to the door around the corner. 'Gentlemen,' it said in block letters, red, like the crosses painted on the sides of ambulances.

'I'll be in the pool,' she said, as she motioned for him to go in. 'Don't jump into the pool if you can't see me.'

Orko hesitated.

'You're a big boy now. It'll be all right. You'll see,' his mother said, her fingers combing his unruly hair to one side.

Orko was about to push the door open when it swung outwards, almost hitting him in the face. A man strode out in his swimming trunks, a gold chain around his neck and a gold watch on his right wrist. Orko made his way past the man. There was another door down a short flight of stairs. Orko opened the door, expecting to find the showers to his left and a neat row of cubicles to his right.

Inside, there were no cubicles. Instead, there was a large hall, lined with benches. The smell reminded him of the doctor's chamber where his mother took him for his shots. There were boys and men everywhere. Two boys laughed as they dried themselves. A young man slapped another on the back. Two men were completely naked. One of the naked men had hair all over his body – on his chest, on his neck, on his knuckles, on his ears, in his crotch. His penis looked shockingly large. He walked about nonchalantly, in no particular hurry to dress himself.

The noise was deafening. Orko wanted to run away, but he couldn't, because he had to be a big boy, and big boys didn't run away. He looked over his shoulder before taking off his T-shirt. He wrapped a towel around his torso, gripping the edges in his armpits. An older boy took off his underwear and stood completely naked, as if to show Orko how it was done. That was when Orko felt the presence. Although he couldn't see it, he was sure that he was being watched by a creature much larger than he was. It smelt of disinfectant. He realised that he couldn't see colours anymore; everything was a shade of grey. He became convinced that this invisible creature, much larger than him, had sucked the colour away. He wondered if he himself had turned grey, when he realised that he couldn't raise his arm. He couldn't move. He could barely breathe.

The naked boy wrapped a towel around his midriff and sauntered off. It was some time before Orko could move again. He hurriedly put his clothes back on. His T-shirt was inside out. He ran from the changing rooms. He didn't stop to fix his shirt because he was scared that the creature would come after him. He ran towards the swimming pool, where the sky was blue. Surely the creature couldn't suck the colour out of the sky.

He waited near the footbath for his mother. When she arrived, in her navy swimming costume and yellow cap, Orko rushed to her in tears. She lifted him up, his head nestling in her breast as he sobbed uncontrollably.

'What happened, Orko? Did someone hurt you?' she asked. Her voice sounded like it did the time when he had come home all bloodied after a tumble from the swing in the playground. He could smell her over the chlorine.

Orko remembers that as the moment when he realised that something was horribly wrong. He had always thought that when he grew up, he would be just like his mother. He did not want hair all over his body, in his armpits, in his crotch. He didn't want to walk bare-chested from the swimming pool, water dripping from his hairy knuckles. If that was how it was going to be, he'd rather not swim.

'I don't want to be a big boy,' he said. 'I want to be like you.'

It was the morning of Orko's eighth birthday, and he had spent the night at Urmi's. They were in her room, playing, when her mother came to fetch him. 'Your grandfather is here,' she said.

Amiya, his maternal grandfather, was at Urmi's doorstep. Orko was surprised when he didn't wish Orko a happy birthday, and he was a little disappointed when he discovered that his grandfather hadn't brought a present.

'We have to leave right away,' Amiya said to him, ruffling his hair.

'Can Urmi come with us?' Orko asked.

'Another time,' his grandfather replied.

They rode in the back seat of Amiya's big black Humber. Orko can't remember who was driving. They were at the crest of a bridge when his grandfather told him that his mother was gone, that the gods had taken her away.

This didn't make sense at all, because Orko's mother was big and strong, and the gods were tiny, made of brass. They sat on the shelf by his mother's dressing table. They couldn't even feed themselves. How could they possibly take his mother away?

'You're lying,' he said to Amiya. 'Ma is much bigger than the gods.'

That was the only time Orko saw a grown man weep.

The next thing Orko remembers is visiting Amiya at the hospital. He remembers thinking that his grandfather's body had deflated, like a balloon. When Amiya tried to smile at him, only the right half of his mouth moved. Orko's father told him later that part of Amiya's brain had stopped working. The doctors said that he had suffered a stroke.

Two

The years following his mother's death are a blur, like a playground seen from a whirling carousel. Breakfast with his father; the ride on the school bus that seemed to finish before it began; books tumbling out of his schoolbag and climbing back in; pages upon pages of notes in his wobbly, indecipherable hand; a different bus on his way back, on a shorter route; Sudeshna, his aunt, at the bus stop, carrying a white umbrella with black polka dots, come rain or shine; lunch with his grandfather, napkins tucked into their collars, lest they soil their shirts. His aunt never ate with them. She said it was more convenient to eat after they had finished.

After lunch, Amiya napped in his armchair while Sudeshna saw to Orko's studies. She taught him long division and multiplication, and she insisted that the tables of thirteen must be recited without the assistance of mental arithmetic. She made sure his homework was done, and she checked his school diary for notes from his teachers. She taught him cursive writing, her hand wrapped around his own tiny hand, guiding the pencil over the dotted lines, making sure he didn't stray or stutter. 'Cursive writing,' she said. 'All civilised people write this way.' Orko could bear it only because he knew that, soon, his grandfather would be awake.

Not given to the banalities that other grown-ups resorted to, Amiya never asked Orko stupid questions. What did he have for breakfast? What did he learn at school that day?

Who was his favourite teacher? What did he want to be when he grew up? Amiya either knew the answers to all those questions or he didn't think they were of any consequence. He never asked Orko to sing *Rabindra Sangeet* or to recite a poem he had learnt at school. After his stroke, his words didn't come out right, and this was a source of constant exasperation for Sudeshna. Orko, on the other hand, had no trouble understanding his grandfather. He clung to every slurred word, wide-eyed with wonder as his grandfather told him stories unlike any he had read. Try as he might, all he can recall about the stories is that there was magic where he was least expecting it.

Beside the TV in his grandfather's house was a signal booster. 'It's a magic box,' he said, when Orko asked him what it was. It sat by the TV, and it was no larger than a loaf of bread. It plucked pictures and words out of thin air. Every afternoon, they watched television from Bangladesh, Amiya's erstwhile homeland. Orko loved the cartoon shows, and he thinks his grandfather did too, because he remembers his grandfather humming the theme from *ThunderCats*.

On Thursdays, Nandan had the afternoon off, and he would arrive shortly after lunch. In the summer, they usually went to the planetarium, or they watched a movie together. Sometimes, when it was really hot, Nandan took Orko back to his office. 'Let's do our homework together,' he would say, with a sheepish grin. Winter afternoons were spent outdoors. Sudeshna packed them a picnic lunch, and Orko went with his father to the Botanic Gardens, or the zoo, or the maidan. Sometimes they just went to the lake.

It was a Thursday, near the end of November. Orko and his father sat astride a bench by the side of the Dhakuria lake. A large plate between them, made from dried sal leaves pinned together, hosted a steadily diminishing stack of sandwiches – some ham, some cheese. It was a bright, pleasant afternoon. Orko followed the languid progress of a rowboat as it made its way across the lake. A man was rowing; a woman sat in the passenger seat, facing the man.

'I'll tell you a story today,' said Nandan. 'It's the story of the biggest boat ever made by mankind.'

Orko kicked off his sneakers and settled in, cross-legged, on the bench.

'It's 1912. Southampton dock,' Nandan started. 'Do you know where Southampton is?'

Orko shook his head.

'In England,' said his father. 'With great fanfare, a ship sets sail. It's a luxury ocean liner, the greatest ever built. Its builders have even gone as far as calling it unsinkable. It's headed for New York, on the other side of the Atlantic Ocean.'

Nandan fished out a pack of cigarettes from his pocket. He lit one, cupping his hands to shield the flame from the gentle breeze blowing across the lake.

'The first four days of the voyage are uneventful. It's on the last night that our story begins. The sky is black, the stars shining through with a brilliance that neither you nor I will see in our lifetimes. Through the vast blackness of sea and sky, the cold steel hull cuts across the surface of the water.'

Orko remembers wondering if his father had read the story in a magazine and learnt it off by heart. The sentences didn't seem like they were constructed offhand, on a November afternoon by the side of a lake.

'The hull is thicker than any the ocean has known before. It conceals a sophisticated system of chambers and air locks, combining to contain the ocean, should it sneak past the ship's first line of defence. On this dark, formidable platform, there appears a row of brilliant lights. Set a little above the first, another row of lights appears. And another. Five. Six. Seven.'

By the time the last row of lights came on, Orko was on board.

'There's a swimming pool,' Nandan continued, 'bigger than the one at the club. There are staterooms and dining halls; in these halls are well-dressed men and women, young and old. Cheeks are pressed together in greeting. Lithe hands gloved in white are kissed. The ship has its own band, and they play on as couples dance on the ballroom floor. Below decks, man and machine combine to keep this giant on schedule. The engine room is gigantic. The boilers are the size of small lorries. The sailors who keep them ticking along are lodged three or four to a cabin the size of our bathroom.'

Just as suddenly as he found himself aboard the vessel, Orko was again a spectator. He was cheering from the sidelines as the behemoth steamed across the North Atlantic.

'Speed is a strange thing,' Nandan said, as he screwed the lid back onto the bottle of tomato sauce. He crushed the plate and threw it into the waters of the lake, before Orko could point out that there was a dustbin just behind him. 'It's perfectly safe for a car to be going twice as fast as the *Titanic* was that night. If you turn a corner and find a fallen tree in your way, you brake. The car digs its heels in, and in the blink of an eye you're at a standstill. All you need to do is back away, turn the car around, and that's that. If a dog bolts across the road, you just turn the steering wheel a little bit, for a fraction of a second. The dog is still alive, and you're on your way. It's between you, your car and the road. There's something solid for the tyres to hold on to. You brake, the wheels lock, the rubber burns against the tarmac. Your car loses energy. You stop. A ship, though, is a different beast.'

Orko knew how propellers worked. 'I know that,' he wanted to say.

'It's almost like running a country,' Nandan continued. 'The captain can't just ride with his hands on the wheel, stepping on the accelerator when he wants to go faster, swerving if another ship appears out of nowhere. Everything has to be plotted and planned well in advance. A ship like that will coast for a couple of kilometres after the captain gives the command to stop. In fact, he can't even see far enough to brake in time to avoid a collision.'

A collision. That was the direction in which the story seemed to be headed.

'It was a grand occasion, whichever way one looks at it. It was the biggest, grandest, most invincible machine ever built. Every evening was a celebration. There was champagne, and there was music. There was dancing, and there were fireworks.'

'Have you ever been on a ship like that?' Orko asked his father.

'I wish,' said Nandan, a faraway look in his eyes. 'The *Titanic* careens through the night. There's the schedule to meet. In addition to being the largest and the grandest, the *Titanic* aspires to be the fastest across the Atlantic.'

Nandan gazed into the distance past Orko. He looked like he was trying to decide how to advance the story.

'And then?' Orko asked, his impatience getting the better of him.

'The North Atlantic is chock-full of icebergs,' his father said. 'A few ships radio warnings to the *Titanic*, but because it's unsinkable the captain isn't particularly worried. As far as the captain is concerned, he is running a tight ship, keeping a diligent watch, marshalling his troops well. The boilers are running at full blast, feeding the ship's engines, keeping the passengers warm in the smoking rooms. The dining is fine. The passengers are happy; some are going home, while others, like the *Titanic*, are on their first run across the Atlantic. For each passenger and crew member, it is a momentous crossing. In the crow's nest, though, is a crewman who has no binoculars.'

The sun had disappeared beyond the curve of the earth, but Orko couldn't see any stars. He heard distant strains of music. It was impossible to pick out the tune, with the cold wind blowing his long, golden hair across his face. There was no one else in sight. The water looked dark and forbidding.

Night fell in the blink of an eye. The moon was conspicuous by its absence. More stars were twinkling than Orko had ever seen, casting their shadowy light on him from the depths of time. The *Titanic*, on the other hand, was just a glittering mass of wood and metal, invisible even from the new moon.

'The ocean is sure to see ships mightier than her, but tonight belongs to the *Titanic*. It's going to be quite a night.' Nandan paused, his eyes settling on a bench on the far side of the lake.

Orko heard a bell as a popcorn seller wheeled his bicycle past their bench. He wasn't hungry. He still could taste the ham and the butter on his palate. He could do with a drink – maybe a glass of cold water. The sky was a giant inky canvas, the stars still points from which he couldn't look away. He shivered when a gust of ocean breeze blew at him. The sea was aglow with an otherworldly light. It was green. Orko grasped the railing and, looking past it, saw luminous streaks below the surface of the ocean, running together, from here to eternity, as if he were on a footbridge over a railway yard, with a distant locomotive shining its light on the tracks that passed below his feet.

'So, everything is just the way it was the night before,' Nandan broke into Orko's private universe. 'Erstwhile strangers exchange addresses. Friendships are forged from the fleeting moments of the voyage. The band begins to wind down, each song less urgent than the one that came before. The man in the crow's nest scans the horizon, and there's nothing to report.'

On his way up to the crow's nest, Orko felt colder with each rung he climbed. When he reached the top, he was greeted by an exhilarating sight. He could see everything from up here – the whole world. There was the peak of K2. He knew the snow-clad summit; he had seen it in a picture on the cover of an issue of *National Geographic*. He took in the sight, his eyes fixed on the mysterious mountain.

When he came to, there was a palpable tension in the air. Something untoward seemed to have happened. Dark figures hurried about with an unmistakable air of urgency. They whispered frantically among themselves, though Orko couldn't hear what they were saying.

'The alarm is raised,' Nandan said, lighting another cigarette. 'The captain of any ship would do well to panic. You must understand that there are about five minutes before the iceberg will be upon them. The wheel is cranked all the way to starboard. It's clear they won't be able to avoid the collision.'

Orko found himself on the boat deck. The passengers still seemed to be oblivious to their impending peril, cocooned in the engineered warmth of the dining room.

'Below decks, the ship is alive with tension. Men scurry about in its bowels, their practised routines ripped to shreds by the unexpected turn of events. The captain is as inscrutable as ever. He has given the commands that are necessary. The ship is fighting its own momentum, straining to change course. The wheel is at the stop.'

There was a sound, like a giant, rusty screw being turned against its will, followed by a mechanical gasp that sounded like the air brakes on a thousand large, dilapidated lorries deploying all at once.

'They've been hit,' said Nandan.

Orko was ahead of the story. He found himself plunging headlong into the frigid waters of the North Atlantic. People were dying all around him. Someone clutched at his slipper, then his dress. He went under, and just as he thought he was going to take on water, his head pierced the surface of the dark ocean. The great ship was listing. Orko went under again. Then there was complete darkness.

For days afterwards, all Orko could think about was broken ships sinking into the world's oceans as thousands of freezing, gasping, drowning people watched in horror. In those weeks, he knew what he wanted to do when he grew up. He would build ships with hulls so invincible that icebergs would just glance off them. The ships would carry thousands of balloons and tanks of helium. If the hull did spring a leak, the balloons would inflate, holding the ship aloft until help arrived.

When Orko laid out this grand design over dinner, his father laughed.

'Modern ships are very safe,' he said. 'Besides, most people fly when they need to travel great distances.'

Some months later, an Air India jet was blown up by terrorists, off the coast of Ireland. The *Emperor Kanishka* had been the largest and grandest of flying machines – a Boeing 747 – and more than three hundred people had been on board. Each one of them was dead.

Orko's father was not surprised. According to him, anyone with a modicum of intelligence should have seen it coming.

A year earlier, the prime minister, Mrs Indira Gandhi, was shot by members of her staff. A complex chain of events unfolded around the tragedy, and Nandan reasoned that the bombing of the *Emperor Kanishka* was retribution for questionable decisions that had been taken at the highest levels of the Indian government. That was all he would say about the matter.

Orko had many questions about all of it, but no one would answer them. Were there members of the government on board the fallen aircraft? The newspapers didn't say so. On the day Mrs Gandhi was assassinated, life came to a standstill in the city. All India Radio and Doordarshan pulled their regular programming. The airwaves were commandeered by a mournful *sarod*, and every few minutes the music would give way to the measured, deferential diction of the newscaster, who gave increasingly dire prognoses about the prime minister's condition. Finally, in the afternoon, it was announced that Mrs Indira Gandhi was dead. The nation went into mourning. His aunt Sudeshna wept openly. It stood to reason that if important people had been on board the lost Boeing, something similar would have happened.

Orko obsessed about the *Emperor Kanishka*. It featured prominently in his dreams, and when he was awake he often drifted away, a passenger in a window seat, looking down at the clouds. Through tears in the infinite white beneath him, he would spot the very same ocean that had swallowed up the *Titanic* so many years ago. Just as he spied the green island off to his left, blood was everywhere. The flesh of three hundred passengers melded with molten steel and hurtled earthward. Orko found himself splashing down into the frigid water, eyes wide open.

He badgered his father for books about passenger planes, and Nandan brought him a few from the university library. On Saturdays they scoured the old bookshops on College Street for anything they could find on the subject. When it came to the *Kanishka*, though, Nandan refused to say anything at all. All Orko knew was what he read in a magazine as he waited to see the doctor.

It was a Friday evening, and Nandan's friend Kundan was visiting them. He often came to their flat on the weekend. After some small talk about school, mathematics and Kundan's vintage Morris Minor, Orko took his chance while his father was in the kitchen.

'Kundan-kaku,' he started. 'Did you hear about the *Emperor Kanishka*?'

Kundan sighed. He looked pensive, and Orko waited eagerly for him to say something about the subject. Kundan gripped the armrests of his chair and dragged himself to the edge of his seat. He stretched out an arm for the ashtray that lay just beyond his reach. Orko handed it to him, and Kundan nestled it in his lap. He fished out a pack of cigarettes from his shirt pocket. He reached back into the pocket for his matchbox, but it wasn't there. He stood up to look in the pockets of his trousers. The empty ashtray clattered to the floor.

Orko fetched a matchbox from the kitchen. Kundan settled back into his chair. He placed a cigarette between his lips and lit it with a flourish. He shook the match to extinguish the flame. He retrieved the fallen ashtray and deposited the burnt matchstick in its mouth. He put the cigarette between his lips and inhaled deeply. Then he pursed his lips and blew smoke through his nostrils. Orko grew increasingly anxious with every passing second. He knew they couldn't have this conversation in his father's presence.

'Well yes. The *Kanishka*,' Kundan finally said, as the last wisps of smoke faded away. 'It was rather sad, wasn't it?'

Orko was taken aback by Kundan's manner, and by his choice of words. He dithered, unsure how to advance the conversation. 'How big is a Boeing 747 anyway?' he asked eventually.

Kundan let out a contrived cough. His manner suggested that he didn't really know, and was embarrassed to admit it. Orko wished he hadn't asked the question. Embarrassing a grown-up was a terrible way to continue a discussion with them. He abandoned the realm of facts and posed a question that would elicit an opinion.

'So is there no chance that anyone survived? They fell into the ocean, didn't they? Some of them must have known how to swim?'

That seemed to strike a chord with Kundan. 'Can you imagine the force of the impact? They were at a height of more than ten kilometres when the aircraft exploded,' he said. 'Mount Everest is a little over twenty-eight thousand feet. This plane was at an altitude of over thirty thousand feet. People die every year climbing Mount Everest – and they don't even have the full height of the mountain to fall through…'

'So they were just presumed dead?' Orko asked, horrified. He imagined scores of passengers struggling to stay alive in freezing waters, with no help on the way.

'I don't think so. Ireland mounted a search and rescue operation – but it was immediately clear that there had been no survivors,' Kundan said, lighting another cigarette.

That didn't seem possible. They did fall into the ocean, after all.

'Did they look everywhere? Like on nearby islands?'

Kundan looked exasperated, like his aunt sometimes did when he took too long to understand a mathematical concept. 'Did you know that most people who climb Mount Everest use oxygen, like scuba divers and astronauts?'

This wasn't something Orko had been aware of. He wondered why Kundan was telling him this. Then it struck him.

'So the plane exploded at a height where there's no oxygen?'

'Well…there is oxygen, right up to sixty thousand feet, and this plane was at thirty thousand or thereabouts. But there certainly isn't enough oxygen up there for a human being to survive,' said Kundan. 'Besides, the cold would have killed them in seconds. Up there, it's colder than it is in Antarctica, and these folks would have been in their shirtsleeves, in the warm cabin of the jumbo.'

The physics was now clear, but the psychology was still a mystery.

'Were there any politicians on board? Someone the bombers were angry with?' Orko asked.

It was at this point that Nandan emerged from the kitchen, with two cups of tea. 'Stop hounding Kundan like that,' he said. 'Why don't you go and finish your homework?'

Usually Orko just left the room when asked to, but this was different. He was having an important discussion, about something that was so confounding that he couldn't have imagined it, had it not actually happened. Besides, Nandan knew that Orko always finished his homework in the afternoon, with his aunt. Nandan had never been summoned to his school, and he had never been sent notes of complaint by Orko's teachers. So the dismissal seemed patently unjust.

'I have done my homework. You know that I have,' Orko said, standing his ground, hoping his father would back off, just until he could have a few more questions answered. His ears felt like someone had taken a hot iron to them. He stood still, on the verge of hyperventilation, his nostrils flaring with each exhalation.

There followed a staring match that Orko lost. He might not have, if Kundan hadn't been watching the standoff, smoking his third cigarette of the evening, its tip glowing as he squinted at Orko through the smoke. Vanquished, Orko retreated to his room. He shut the door behind him and threw himself on his bed. He buried his face in his pillow as he began to shake violently. Then the tears came.

He wouldn't have been as angry as he was if his father's behaviour hadn't been so out of character. Nandan seldom talked down to Orko, and he never dismissed Orko's questions as impertinent. When it came to the *Kanishka*, though, he had been devilishly evasive. What was more, he didn't seem to be suitably shocked about it. When Orko asked him why someone would deliberately blow up an aeroplane, he told Orko the story of the Golden Temple in the state of Punjab, and about Mrs Indira Gandhi, their late prime minister, who sent her troops into the holy sanctum. He followed it up with a rant about the evils of organised religion. At the end of it, Orko's question still remained unanswered: what did the people on board the aeroplane have to do with all of that?

Over the next few days, a devastating idea took shape in Orko's mind. It crept in surreptitiously, perhaps in a dream. His father knew who had blown up the Boeing, and he had known all along when they were going to do it. That was why he wasn't surprised when it happened. Seemingly unrelated facts began to come together, like the pieces of a puzzle, and suddenly everything made sense. His father had been in Japan recently, where a bag had exploded at Tokyo's Narita airport, killing two airport employees. He had a close friend in Ludhiana, and that, Orko knew, was in Punjab. A quick look at the atlas told Orko that it wasn't very far from Amritsar, where the Golden Temple was located. He wondered if Kundan was in on it too. Like his father, Kundan had tried to put off talking about the *Kanishka*, with that show of lighting his cigarette, hoping, perhaps, that Nandan would rescue him before things got out of hand.

Orko couldn't bring himself to talk to anyone about his horrible secret, and because it was always on his mind he stopped talking to his friends at school; he spoke to his teachers only when there was no way around it. At home, he remained silent unless spoken to. Every night he tossed and turned, shuffling through the horrifying sequence of events, until he fell into a dreamless sleep. This went on for close to a month, and by the end of it he could take no more. He decided that he had to talk to someone about it all, if only to have them tell him that he was crazy.

It was a Monday. Orko remembers this because they had class tests on Mondays, and on that particular Monday Orko had been unable to answer a single question. Afterwards, when his aunt met him at the bus stop, he didn't meet her gaze, because he was afraid that he might begin to cry.

At lunch, he sat at Amiya's side, faint with anxiety, unable to eat a single morsel. He had to talk to someone, and the only person he could trust was his grandfather.

'Dadu,' he began, just as Amiya was settling in for his nap. 'What would you do if someone you knew did something terrible?'

'How terrible?' Amiya asked.

'Really bad. Something that killed hundreds of people,' Orko said. His fists were clenched, and he felt the tips of his fingers pulse in time with the frantic beating in his breast.

'Do you know someone like that? Someone bragging that it was he who blew up that plane, perhaps?' Amiya asked, the slightest hint of a smile twinkling at the corners of his eyes.

Orko's first instinct was to bolt. He hadn't thought Amiya would decipher his foggy allusion so easily. It was almost as if he had read Orko's mind. He fought the urge to run away, and collected his thoughts as best he could.

'Well, he didn't blow it up,' he said. 'He was here when it happened...but I think he knows who did.'

Amiya ruffled Orko's hair and took his hand. For a while, they said nothing.

'Who are we talking about here?'

Orko couldn't answer the question without giving it all away. He wasn't sure if Amiya had guessed that it was his father. For the first time he began to have doubts, and he had half a mind to tell his grandfather that he had been speaking hypothetically.

'He won't talk about it,' he blurted out, unable to contain himself. 'He won't let me talk to anyone else. He says it was all right for the bombers to do what they did – that they had their reasons.'

'So you're only guessing,' Amiya said after a moment's pause.

Orko was indignant. 'Of course I'm not guessing. I know.'

He couldn't bring himself to say any more. He had struggled to fall asleep the night before, a hapless spectator as his mind shuffled through the possible consequences of divulging his terrible secret. The scenario that seemed the most likely involved the police hauling his father off to prison, with Orko placed in his aunt's care, learning his tables and practising cursive writing all day, every day, until he was old enough to get a job.

Amiya put his arm around Orko's shoulders. 'Your father forgets that you're a child,' he said under his breath. 'You should talk to him,' he continued. 'You must demand answers. Refuse to go away until you have them. You mustn't jump to conclusions.'

'I did ask him,' said Orko. 'He won't talk about it.'

Then he thought of something that he was sure would get his grandfather's attention.

'He says there are no gods. There's no one pulling on strings to control our lives, and there's no one to punish us in an afterlife. He says it's all superstition, invented by the ancients to explain the sun, the moon, the stars, rain and thunder. Now that we know what causes all of that, we don't need gods anymore.'

It all came out in a breathless jumble, and when he finished, Amiya appeared to consider his statement carefully. 'What does all of this have to do with the aeroplane?' he asked.

Orko struggled to join the dots. 'Well…I don't know,' he said. 'I've told you everything. You decide.'

'There are three sides to every story,' Amiya said. Orko couldn't be sure if he was speaking to himself, like he often did. 'Sometimes, when we're angry, we tend to close the windows of our minds. We only see our side of the story, and we jump to conclusions that couldn't be further from the truth.'

'Three sides?'

'Well…let's take your story of this aeroplane, for instance. You are a young boy. This is possibly the most horrific thing you've ever known to happen – am I right?'

Orko nodded.

'You've been thinking about it all the time…wondering why someone would send all those innocent people to their deaths…what could possibly make them so angry. You probably even have nightmares…'

'Yes,' Orko said. 'I often dream that I'm in the plane, and then it explodes, and then I'm drowning…'

'Why do you think that your father had something to do with it?' Amiya's tone was gentle.

'He said that Mrs Gandhi sent the army into the Golden Temple, and then two of her bodyguards shot her. Then, because the bodyguards were Sikh, people burned down the houses of Sikhs who had nothing to do with the killing, and the government did nothing to stop them.' Even as Orko reeled off all of this, he struggled to make the connection with the *Kanishka*. 'And then he said that religion is the root of all evil, and that idols, temples, mosques and churches are playthings for adults…' He was growing even more muddled as he tried to piece everything together. Then he remembered the clincher: 'He has a friend in Ludhiana, and he was in Japan just before that other bag blew up at the airport.'

'Well,' said Amiya, 'these are things that happen to be true, and they do seem to fit in nicely with your side of the story.' From his manner, Orko could sense that his grandfather was not persuaded by his argument. 'There's another side of the story – the only one that's indisputably true,' Amiya said. 'Someone placed a bomb in the aeroplane – we may never know why. The bomb exploded, killing everyone on board. The death of so many people was not an Act of God, and it was not carried out by demons from the underworld. It was another human like you and me, who decided to end the lives of all those poor people.'

Amiya paused for a sip of water. A few drops dribbled down his chin. Orko handed him a napkin. Amiya raised it to his lips, his fingers trembling as he struggled to wipe off the drops of water.

'But there are thousands and thousands of people in the world,' Orko said, after his grandfather put the napkin away. 'They all think different things. Aren't those thousands of sides to the same story?'

'Well...they don't know that Orko here thinks his father is in cahoots with bombers, do they? So they don't even know this story. The story is entirely yours.' Amiya smiled at Orko. 'So, there's your side, and your father's side. The third side, my dear Orko, is the truth.'

Orko mulled it over for a moment. It still didn't make sense. 'Okay,' he said. 'This story has three sides. What about something that has nothing to do with me? Does that story have three sides too?'

'Let's see,' his grandfather said, the smile reappearing on his lips. 'For instance, your father says there are no gods, no afterlife, and that nothing willed the universe into existence. It's all down to time and physics. Right?'

Orko nodded.

'Your mother, on the other hand, was of a different persuasion. She didn't deny the physics – but she didn't think it told the whole story. She found it fascinating that the entire universe had to work together, in perfect harmony, to make life possible. There had to be something that kept it all in tune. A truth-keeper. A curator, responsible for the beauty that surrounds us.'

Orko interrupted his grandfather: 'Do gods exist, or don't they?'

'Well. I haven't seen any gods. Do you know the story of Ramakrishna Paramhansa?'

Orko nodded. Sudeshna had read to him from an anthology that chronicled the saint's life.

'He had visions of the goddess Kali. He had conversations with her. His life is well documented. There doesn't seem to be any motive for him to have lied. He's not the only one. There are people all over the world who have had supernatural experiences of some sort. There's no way for us to climb into their skin and judge for ourselves, but in an overwhelming majority of cases there wasn't anything to be gained from lying about the experience.' Amiya paused. 'But I have to admit – I don't know if gods exist. I think they do, but I don't know.'

Orko felt let down. He had hoped for a firm answer from his grandfather. He remembered that this had been a mere digression; they had been talking about his father and the aeroplane. He could always return to this later.

'So what's the third side of this story?' he asked.

'The third side…is, as usual, the truth,' Amiya said. 'The gods either are or they are not. It doesn't matter one jot what either of us believes. Some claim to have seen gods of various kinds. Others dismiss these claims as delusions. None of that really matters. Time marches on. The planets go around the sun. You and I sit here discussing gods and aeroplanes, and we don't know the first thing about either.'

They sat quietly for a while. Orko felt dejected. He shuffled the puzzle around in his mind. He had missed something. It was as clear as day to him. How could his grandfather dismiss the whole thing out of hand?

Then he remembered.

'Don't you see – he could do this only because he thinks that he won't be punished in his next life,' he said triumphantly.

His grandfather had fallen asleep.

The next day, Sudeshna picked Orko up from the bus stop, as usual. He had lunch with his grandfather, their napkins tucked into their collars. Orko did his homework while Amiya napped in his chair.

Amiya woke at four-thirty. Sudeshna served him his tea, with his quota of two thin arrowroot biscuits. It was cloudy, and the TV reception was incredibly clear. The ThunderCats went about their business, in pursuit of the villain of the week. Just when it was becoming really interesting, the TV fell silent and the ceiling fan began to run out of steam.

'This is so unfair!' Orko exclaimed.

His grandfather was quiet. Orko looked towards him, to see if he had fallen asleep. Amiya's eyes were open, but he didn't respond when Orko called out to him. His body seemed completely still. He nudged his grandfather, but Amiya didn't react. Orko ran to fetch his aunt. She felt for her father's pulse and, without a trace of emotion, rang for the doctor. 'Please come,' was all he heard her say. She ushered Orko out of the room. She told him that her father was very sick, and Orko should go and play outside. There was no urgency in her manner. Instinctively, Orko knew that his grandfather had died.

The first thoughts that came to Orko revolved around the unfinished conversation of the day before. He wondered if Amiya could still read his mind. His father had told him that when people died, they just stopped existing. There were no spirits, and there certainly was no afterlife. The body was just an agglomeration of organic matter that could no longer process food or oxygen, and if left alone, it began to decompose.

Sudeshna, on the other hand, told him that when people died, the spirit lingered among their loved ones until it had been convinced, by way of various rituals and appeasements of the gods, that it must depart. A virtuous life meant that the spirit would be reborn in a good family, and would prosper in the next innings. A life of sin would result in rebirth as a dog, or a jackal, or even a cockroach.

Orko didn't really know if he believed his father's version or his aunt's. Complete annihilation on one hand, and an endless cycle of reincarnations on the other. He was desperate for a sign of some sort, to help him decide one way or the other. Surely the power cut was no coincidence? His grandfather had smiled at him just a few moments before he died. Was the power cut of his design, to draw Orko's attention away from the television screen? Orko wanted to believe that his grandfather still existed, in some form, and that he would come back. He had been the best human being Orko had ever known. It seemed unjust that he would simply cease to exist. He was convinced his grandfather would not be reborn as a dog or a cockroach. If Orko led a virtuous life, maybe he would be reborn as Amiya's granddaughter the next time around. He wondered how much time he had before the rituals were carried out. He made a mental list of all the things that he wanted to say, of all the questions he wanted answers to. It occurred to him that he could ask away all he wanted; his grandfather would no longer be able to reply. That was when he began to cry.

After Amiya died, Orko remained alert, hoping to meet his grandfather's ghost. He wondered if the ghost would recognise him. Would it remember their conversations? Would he be frightened, if, in fact, he did come face to face with it? He was prepared for every scenario he had come across in the myriad ghost stories his father had told him, but there was no ghost to be found.

Was it possible that his grandfather had forgotten him? There was no one in the world that Orko loved more than he did his grandfather, but he couldn't assume that he was the most important person in his grandfather's life. Amiya had turned seventy-two on his last birthday. Seventy-two years was a very long time – longer than Orko could imagine. Surely, in his long life, his grandfather had made many friends. Perhaps he was visiting them first. He was sure Amiya would come back to him to say goodbye. He just had to be patient.

Because of their last conversation, Orko's memories of his grandfather became inextricably entangled with the horror of the bombed aircraft. He kept replaying that truncated conversation in his mind. The indictment that had seemed so compelling at the time now seemed like a jumble of facts that didn't really belong together.

Orko tried to form a mental picture of the people who planted the bomb on the aircraft, but he failed to fit his father into that mould. It didn't add up. He imagined the bombers as really angry people. They had to be, to plan the deaths of so many people. His father, on the other hand, was a kind, gentle man. Orko had never seen him cry, or become violently angry. Someone like his father could never sympathise with people who blew up aeroplanes. He felt silly for having tortured himself for so many months. He wished he hadn't troubled his grandfather with his fantastic conjecture. He knew he had caused his grandfather anguish. Maybe he had even hastened Amiya's demise.

The truth was that he had been angry with his father for refusing to talk about the *Kanishka*. He didn't understand how his father could be stoic about something so horrific. When his father shooed him away just as he was about to have a conversation with Kundan, he felt belittled.

He still was angry with his father. He didn't feel like he owed his father an apology. If Nandan hadn't been so devoid of emotion, Orko would never have imagined that he was in cahoots with bombers. It had been horribly unpleasant; he could barely speak to his classmates or his teachers, lest he inadvertently betray his father.

He thought about the war movies he had watched with Kundan, and he wished the wars that gave birth to the movies had never happened. He wished everyone was like his grandfather: capable of seeing three sides of every story.

A few months after Amiya's passing, Sudeshna announced that she was going away to Dehradun, to tend to unfinished business. Before she left, she handed Orko a large box wrapped in old newspaper, sealed with sticky tape. The box had his name on it, written in a familiar shaky hand. In the box, Orko found a stack of notebooks, tied together with twine.

In the top right corner of the first page of each notebook was his mother's name, and the year. The years were long ago, markers of time that had passed before he was born.

Some of the early notebooks had the words 'Private' or 'Keep Out' written in the centre of the first page. Orko had notebooks like these. In them, he wrote things that he wouldn't tell anyone. They were private. He would be aghast if his father, or Urmi, or even his grandfather knew the things he had written in them. He couldn't possibly read his mother's notebooks. He wondered if his grandfather had read them.

With the notebooks was a faded black-and-white picture of his mother, dressed in a saree. She was sitting on a bench. The bench was probably somewhere in the park by the side of the lake, but the picture had too little detail to suggest exactly where it was.

At the bottom of the box was a little black volume. It was hardbound, a little smaller and thicker than his mother's notebooks. The front cover had no title – just a heart, engraved in silver. The title page had an inscription in his mother's writing. His mother's name and his grandfather's surname. He imagined his name followed by his grandfather's surname. He liked his mother's name more than he liked his own.

Over the next few days Orko read the book many times, never tiring of it. The Happy Prince. The Nightingale and the Rose. The Remarkable Rocket. The Devoted Friend. The stories cast a spell over him, and he felt as if he knew the author intimately, and that the stories were written especially for him. He put the book away only because he didn't want to wear out the yellowing pages.

When Urmi's mother learned that Sudeshna was going away, she convinced Nandan that Orko was too young to spend all that time alone in an empty flat. He could have lunch with Urmi, and they could finish their homework together. Afterwards, they could go out and play.

'Thank you very much, Ketakidi,' his father said, as they stood to take their leave. 'You've taken a great weight off my shoulders.'

Orko should have been happy; after all, Urmi was his best friend. By then, though, he had begun to envy her, for things that would seem frivolous to most people. The earrings. The pretty clothes. The dance classes. Sometimes the envy drowned out every other emotion, and left him feeling unworthy, friendless and desolate.

Three

Gariahat literally means 'the market of Garia'. Tens of thousands of people shop here every day, for vegetables, fish, fruits, mutton, stationery, tea, underwear. The footpaths that lead to the market are lined with shops that sell books and toys, sweetmeats and shoes and kitchen utensils. There are jeweller's shops, where quiet old men sit behind iron bars with their magnifying glasses and their tiny scales, and there are hole-in-the-wall shops that repair broken food processors and wristwatches. At the junction is a megastore that sells television sets, refrigerators, stereo systems, toasters and ovens.

The most abundant, though, are the shops that sell clothing, costume jewellery and cosmetics. They do a brisk business all year round, but in the festive season they go into overdrive. There are throngs of people on the footpaths – women, mostly, walking at a leisurely pace. The shopkeepers vie for their attention.

'*Mashima!*' they call out to the older, matronly women. Orko's mother would probably qualify as *boudi*. Girls Orko's age, or a little older, are *didimoni*. In this sea of humanity, Orko is less than human. No one calls out to him. No one ever tries to sell him anything. They hurry him along if he stops in his tracks.

He dawdles by a newsstand, carelessly thumbing through a sports weekly. Across the footpath, perched precariously on the curb, is a shanty, fashioned out of salvaged asbestos siding and discarded packing crates. The makeshift counter is covered by a blue tarpaulin. Spread out on the counter are cardboard boxes containing lipstick, eyeliner, hairclips and bottles of nail polish. Above the counter, strung out on lengths of twine, are earrings. They're mounted, like a lepidopterist's butterflies, on white cardboard squares about half the size of a business card. There are simple studs, gold and silver, set with rubies and emeralds and topaz. Some are elaborate, shaped like tiny chandeliers, designed to dangle tantalisingly by the jawbone. The ones Orko likes best are the long, simple earrings, made of wooden beads dyed crimson and ochre and green.

A few weeks ago, Orko and Urmi had stopped at this stall on their way home. They had a tutorial after school, so Urmi couldn't take the school bus. They left school together, Urmi and Orko. He wanted to take Fern Road, but she insisted they come this way.

As they passed the shanty, the man in charge called out to Urmi. '*Didimoni*! Here! Two pairs, for just thirty rupees!'

Urmi bought a pair fashioned out of colourful beads, and another, made from oxidised metal, with tiny dragonflies dangling at the tips. Orko was breathless. Memories rushed in, like a gust of wind before a rainstorm. The bustle of Gariahat faded away, and they were seven years old again. Urmi had just had her ears pierced, and she wore a pair of gold earrings that were just large enough to go around the bottom of her earlobe and back again to the perforation.

'Can I have earrings like Urmi's?' Orko remembers asking his mother.

'Earrings? But you're a boy, and boys don't wear earrings,' his mother said.

'I'm not a boy,' he said. That was the first time he remembers saying it.

'Of course you're a boy,' his mother replied.

'Please?' he persisted. 'I just want one pair, like Urmi's.'

'You should make friends with other boys,' his mother said to him. 'Playing with Urmi all the time isn't doing you any good. Let me see if I can get you into that football camp during the summer holidays.'

Orko let the matter go, because he didn't want to play football. He thought it was silly, kicking a ball from one end of the field to the other. It wasn't fair. Urmi didn't have to play football.

That night, he prayed to Ma Lokkhi, to turn him into a girl, just like Urmi. As he fell asleep, he imagined the two of them playing in her room. He was wearing a frock that belonged to him, and earrings just like hers. He was going to need a new name. Maybe his mother could help him with that.

When he awoke the next morning, he ran his fingers through his hair, even before he was fully awake. He was disappointed when it felt familiar: short, rough, bristly near the back of his neck. He felt his earlobes, but there were no holes. He ran to the mirror, and was heartbroken. Ma Lokkhi hadn't granted his wish. He wondered if it was because everyone thought he was a boy; if Ma Lokkhi turned him into a girl, she would then have to secretly meddle with other people's memories.

That was when he began to fear that he was stuck being a boy. He wasn't going to grow up and be like his mother. He was never going to wear a dress, or a saree. He would never have earrings. The despair he felt was tinged with envy, and that envy has remained with him, rearing its ugly head when he least expects it. Sometimes it's bigger than him, and it wraps itself around him until he can't breathe. It even has a colour, and it isn't green; it's burnt sienna.

'Why don't you take up football?' Orko's father said to him out of the blue one day. 'You'll make new friends. Besides, a boy your age should play a team sport. It builds character.'

The sports club in their neighbourhood ran a coaching program at the club grounds. It was just a few minutes from their flat. 'I've made enquiries,' his father said. 'The coach is excellent. He's agreed to take you, even though you're already fourteen. He says you should be able to catch up if you make the effort.'

Orko and Urmi passed the club sometimes, when they went cycling in the afternoon. They never stopped there, for there was always a game or two of football going on. The boys on the field looked older than them. They were all bigger than them. They were loud, and they were muddy from the tumbles they took on the field.

'What fun,' Urmi said when she heard about the football camp. Orko knew she wasn't being sincere, because they had talked about football before, and they both thought it was violent and silly.

In the end he agreed to go, because the football camp was only for boys. Urmi took dance lessons, and when he asked her if he could come too, she laughed. 'You'd look really silly,' she said. 'Besides, there are no boys in the class.' This was Orko's chance to get even with her. He was going to pretend that he had changed his mind about football.

He would tell Urmi how much he enjoyed it, and he would brag about his footballing prowess. When she expressed interest, he would taunt her. He would laugh at her, and tell her that girls could never play football as well as boys, and she shouldn't bother trying.

On the first day of the camp, Orko was relieved to find that some of the boys were close to him in age. They were not as intimidating as the older boys he had seen when he cycled past the field. Bishu Bhowmick, their coach, had been in the state football squad before Orko was born. He was a hulk of a man, with a head of unruly hair and a thick moustache. He had broad shoulders, and his upper arms were as thick as lampposts. His calf muscles pulsed when he ran. Even his large belly looked like it was made of solid muscle. His booming voice sent a shiver down Orko's spine.

The early days weren't too bad. Orko learned to head, kick and dodge. He was able to run twenty laps around the football field, and he was only a little winded afterwards. The coach often praised Orko for his skill and his stamina. The boys, on the other hand, began to tease him. Everything about him was wrong, apparently – the way he walked, the way he talked, the way he crossed his legs when he sat down. They asked him why he didn't wear a frock. They pushed him and they shoved him when he protested. It wasn't pleasant at all, but it was no worse than he had imagined it would be. The coach intervened sometimes, but not often enough.

'It's great fun,' he said to Urmi a week after he joined the camp. He repeated the coach's words of praise, with considerable embellishment. Urmi was happy for him, but she still didn't show any interest in football. So he told her about his new friends. 'We're going for a movie,' he said when she asked him if he wanted to study together on Saturday. 'I wish you could come too, but you'll probably feel a little left out when we talk about football.'

It was three weeks into the camp when everything changed. On the day, he reached the football field a little later than usual, he cannot remember why. Bishu wasn't there yet. The two boys that he liked the least pointed at him and smirked. As soon as he was within earshot, it started.

'Out of my way, silly cow,' said Neel, in a singsong voice.

'Or I'll pelt you with flowers,' Arijit piped in, pursing his lips.

Orko usually ignored them when they did that, but that day he saw the creature again, the one that sucked the colour out of everything. The turf was grey. The boys were grey. The houses around the football field were grey. He didn't dare look up at the sky to see if it was still blue. He couldn't bear it. He wanted to fight the creature, to defeat it, once and for all.

He let out a war cry and charged at the boys. He kicked and punched, scratched and bit indiscriminately, stopping only when he felt a hand inside his shorts, followed by a numbing pain that emanated from his groin. It knocked the wind out of him. It travelled upwards to his stomach, and downwards to his thighs. He fell to the ground and curled up, unable to breathe.

'He's grown a pair,' laughed Neel. The others joined in.

'Orka's grown a pair of balls,' they said, in a singsong voice. Somebody let out a guffaw and kicked him in the shin. The whole time, Orko hoped nobody he knew would witness this humiliation.

The boys would have continued to kick him if Saikat hadn't intervened. Saikat was the oldest boy at the camp. He was taller than the rest of them, and he had the deepest, most imposing voice. 'Leave him alone,' he said calmly, just like a grown-up would, and the boys scattered as though the words were a magic spell.

Although Orko could breathe again, his whole body ached. The coach arrived just as he was beginning to gather himself.

'Are you all right?' he asked.

'Sir,' cried Orko. 'They…'

He couldn't bring himself to utter the words, and Bishu didn't wait for him to finish his sentence. 'Stop crying,' he said as he led Orko towards the goalpost, where the rest of the boys were. 'I'll talk to you after practice.'

Bishu clapped his hands and blew his whistle, calling them all to attention. He divided the squad into two teams. They were adversaries now, lined up like pawns on a chessboard before the start of play. Every time the coach looked at him, Orko looked away. He was sure he was going to be expelled, or severely reprimanded. After all, he had thrown the first punch.

'Sit,' Bishu said to them. He paced between the lines, surveying his charges. Finally, he stationed himself as if the boys were seated at a table, and he at its head. There was a ball at his feet and a whistle on a bright yellow lanyard around his neck. He stood, arms akimbo, the tip of his boot on the ball, like the statue of a famous footballer Orko had once seen, though he could not remember where.

'Football,' he said, 'has two simple objectives. First – get the ball between the opponent's goalposts, as many times as you can. That is to say, score goals. In torrents.'

Two boys sitting across from Orko whispered to one another. One of them raised his palm across his face to hide a smirk. Bishu glared at the errant boys until they took notice. Moisture from the grass seeped through the seat of Orko's shorts.

'The second objective is more difficult than the first,' he continued. 'You have to keep your opponents away from your goalposts. If you can't, you'll lose.'

The coach was right. The objectives were simple. Score goals. Don't let the opponents score any. On the other hand, the whole endeavour seemed asinine. How did so many people all over the world find this fascinating?

'Individual brilliance is, of course, beautiful to watch,' the coach went on. 'But individuals don't win games. Teams win games. You need to have unity of thought. The most important aspect of the game is team spirit.'

With that, he blew his whistle and clapped his hands again. The boys stood up. The coach directed them to their positions on the field, and the ball was in play.

The boys ran up and down the field, jostling for the ball, tripping each other, sometimes deliberately, between frantic bursts from the whistle. Orko remained rooted to the spot assigned to him. He wasn't sure what was expected of him. He could try to get at the ball and take it forward, maybe even have a shot at the goal, but he saw six others doing exactly that. He could go down towards the goal he was supposed to defend, but there was no one there except the goalkeeper. His eyes followed the ball as it went back and forth across the centre line. When someone kicked it out of play, the coach walked over to Orko and asked him if anything was the matter. Orko shook his head and ran off in the general direction of the action.

For the rest of the afternoon, he stayed close to the ball, but the only contact he made with it was when a shot from one of the boys ricocheted off his shoulder. He even forgot which team he was on. He was glad when the long whistle signalled the end of play.

'Your mind was not on the game today,' the coach said to Orko after practice.

Orko couldn't bring himself to respond. He was sure Bishu had seen the boys kick him and call him names. He was ashamed, because this never happened to anybody else. The boys often fooled around, but it was all in good humour. They never ganged up on anyone else the way they ganged up on him. What was most unbearable was that so many of them sat around and watched, as if it was just a game. Tears began to come, and it was all he could do to fight them back.

'You don't like that they pick on you, do you?' Bishu asked. His voice sounded softer and kinder than it had earlier in the afternoon. For the first time, he seemed to be on Orko's side.

Orko shook his head.

'Well, I used to be bullied too,' Bishu said, almost in a whisper, and Orko began to sob. This seemed to fluster Bishu. 'I don't think you should continue with the camp,' he said.

Orko's heart sank. His worst fears were coming true: he was being expelled. Siddharth had been expelled from his school a few years ago. He was a horrid boy. He beat up the younger children and swore at one of their teachers. His parents were summoned to the principal's office countless times before he was finally asked to leave. The thought of being expelled was more shameful than Orko could bear. He couldn't believe this was happening, and in that moment he forgot how much he detested the football camp. He wanted to remain, at all costs.

'But I didn't do anything at all,' he said. 'They were calling me names. They were the ones who hit me.' He was surprised by the alacrity with which he said these words, because they weren't true. He had thrown the first punch.

'Some of the boys find your manner very distracting,' Bishu said.

Orko was dumbfounded. He had put his heart and soul into football these past few weeks. He had paid attention to Bishu's instructions. He couldn't think of anything he had done that was extraneous or unnecessary. Bishu himself had praised him on many occasions. He hung his head, unable to respond to Bishu's accusation.

'I think you need to change a few basic things,' Bishu said. 'I can help you.'

Orko saw a glimmer of hope; maybe all was not lost. He waited for Bishu to tell him what he needed to work on, but Bishu said nothing.

As he turned to go, Bishu called after him. 'There's no time to lose. Why don't you come home with me? We can start your lessons today.'

Orko was taken by surprise. 'Okay,' was all he could say.

They walked to the cycle stand at the back of the clubhouse. Bishu took a set of keys from the pocket of his shorts and unlocked a large green bicycle. He wheeled it out of the parking area and mounted. He took his left hand off the handlebars and indicated, with a nod of his head, that Orko should sit on the crossbar.

'It's not very far. We'll be able to talk freely,' Bishu said, before they began rolling.

They went past the football field and down an earthen track that was just wide enough for the bicycle. After about half a kilometre, Bishu leaned into a left turn; his belly rubbed against Orko's side. They went past houses, single-storey with tiled roofs that were once brick-red. Many were fronted by fences and wicker gates fashioned out of bamboo. Some had plantain or guava trees growing in front. The street was deserted. A solitary crow cawed in the distance. The pedals squeaked with every revolution. Orko was reminded of a ghost town, from a story his father told him years ago.

After a few minutes, they came to a halt. 'Here we are,' said Bishu.

Orko slid off the crossbar. He was a little sore, but he didn't know if it was from the beating he had taken or from sitting on the crossbar of Bishu's bicycle. The house stood on a large plot surrounded by a shoulder-high brick wall. At its centre was a little red gate. Bishu dismounted and undid the latch. He pulled the gate outwards and wheeled his bicycle in. Orko followed, though he was not sure that he should.

The plot was neatly bisected by a narrow concrete strip that led from the gate to the front door. To the right was a tubewell. To the left, in a patch of grass, was a clump of trees of varying shapes and sizes. Orko recognised a palm tree, a plantain and a guava tree, among others that he couldn't name.

The house wasn't very big. It looked like it had no more than two rooms. The walls were pink. The window frames were lime-green, their frosted panes embossed with a floral pattern.

Bishu parked his bicycle by the tubewell and made for a flight of stairs to the right of the house. Orko stood by the bicycle.

'Come on,' Bishu said, and motioned for Orko to follow him.

The staircase was narrow. It was a single flight, with an unpainted iron guardrail. From the terrace, Orko saw that there was a pond at the back of the house. A concrete stairway descended into its murky waters. The pond was surrounded by overgrown, haphazard shrubbery. On the far side was a dark thicket of tall trees.

On the terrace, tucked away in a corner, was a small room, its walls the colour of unpainted concrete. The windows were the same colour and design as the ones downstairs. The door was secured by a padlock hanging off a deadbolt. Bishu dug into the zippered pocket of his football shorts and retrieved his keys.

Inside the room was a writing table with a matching chair, a single bed and a large bookshelf, full of trophies and medals. The medals were enclosed in a glass case, against a green felt background. The walls were plastered with photographs of Bishu, mostly in black and white. Some were mounted on frames, others pasted on green chart paper. In one photo he was standing with a football in the crook of his arm. In another he was on the podium, accepting a trophy from an important-looking man with white hair. In yet another he was posing with his team, on his knees, smiling, young, maybe just a few years older than the oldest boys in the coaching camp.

'That's my first match with the state team,' Bishu said, a wistful smile on his face. 'I played more than a thousand games. No one would have thought…' His voice trailed off. 'You can be a great footballer too,' he said to Orko. 'Before you can do that, though, you have to earn the respect of your teammates.'

Orko felt indignant. Just a few days ago the coach had said that he had a natural ability, and Orko had worked hard, in spite of the fact that he hated football. It was all going well until they started that nonsense about the cows and the flowers. Something snapped inside of him as he relived the humiliation of the afternoon.

'I don't want to play with them,' he blurted out. 'They're horrid. They tease me and call me names.' He regretted the words the moment they left his lips. He hoped Bishu wouldn't take umbrage. He didn't want to be expelled from the camp. He felt his eyes well up with tears again. Before he knew it, he was sobbing.

'That's what you need to work on first,' said Bishu. 'You're not a girl. You can't dissolve in a puddle of tears at the drop of a hat.'

Orko wiped his tears away. He took a deep breath, like his mother had taught him to. As his sobs receded, the anger welled up again.

'They can't treat me like this,' he said. 'They tease me. I've never said a word to either of them. They just won't leave me alone.'

'They're good boys,' said Bishu. 'This is quite normal. If you can't face this, how will you face life when you grow up? The world is not a doll's house, you know!'

There was an edge in Bishu's voice, and Orko's heart skipped a beat. Did Bishu know that he had played with dolls, once upon a time? Was that going to be held against him? Did Bishu bring him home just to tell him that he had to leave the camp? Was he going to tell Orko's father?

'Maybe you should come back to the football camp next year,' Bishu continued. 'This year, I'll teach you some other things.' He walked out of the room and onto the terrace. Orko followed him outside.

'Do you have an older sister?' Bishu asked him, as they stood there on the terrace.

Orko was taken aback. 'No,' he said tentatively. 'I am an only child.'

'And your parents? Does your father live in another city?'

'I live with my father. My mother passed away,' said Orko.

'Oh. I'm sorry to hear that,' said Bishu. 'How old were you then?'

'Eight.'

Bishu stared at Orko, as if he were a curiosity. Orko stood still, confused. Bishu paced about, looking pensive. When he stopped pacing, his face was uncomfortably close to Orko's.

'Do you have any friends at all?' he asked.

'I have lots of friends at school,' Orko replied.

'Who is your best friend?'

'Urmi. She is in my class, and she lives right next door.'

'And your other friends? Are they all girls?' There was a hint of derision in Bishu's voice. Suddenly he seemed just like the boys on the football field.

'No,' Orko said defiantly. 'Sugato and Bodhi are boys.'

Sugato was in Orko's class. He had excellent handwriting, and he took very good notes in class. He was quiet and diligent, and during the lunch break he was usually at the library. Orko had malaria last year, and had missed two weeks of school. When he returned, Sugato helped him catch up with the rest of the class. Bodhi wasn't really Orko's friend. He was Urmi's older brother, and he often advised Orko about how he should conduct himself at school.

'Do you really want to play football?' Bishu asked, his voice gentle and calm again.

Orko did not want to play football. He did not want to have anything to do with it. He hated the sport, and he hated the boys he had to deal with every day. He would rather do his homework with Urmi. If he discontinued, though, she was going to ask him why he wasn't going to the football ground anymore, and he would have to admit to her that it had all been a lie, and that he really hated football.

'Yes, sir. I want to play football,' he said, trying his best to sound determined. Bishu was quiet. He looked away from Orko, into the distance past the pond at the back of the house. Orko was beginning to feel really anxious. He fidgeted with the hem of his shorts. Several minutes seemed to pass before Bishu spoke again.

'You have skill, and stamina. But that isn't all football is about. When you walk out on the field, your opponents size you up very quickly, and if you appear weak, they will target you. Your teammates need to know that they can depend on you.'

'But they can, sir,' said Orko. He felt ashamed about the way he had been on the field that day. 'I was a little distracted today,' he said, hoping that was explanation enough. He couldn't think of anything he had done before that day that would give people the impression that he couldn't be depended upon.

Bishu shook his head. 'They don't take you seriously because you have a disease,' he said. 'You walk like a girl, and you start crying at the slightest provocation.'

Orko wasn't sure what Bishu meant. He thought of the boys and girls in his class. They all had their individual gaits, but basically they all put one foot before the other, to get where they wanted to be. Did boys and girls really walk differently? Did he walk like a girl?

Bishu went back into the room and came back with a square of blue tailor's chalk. He drew two lines on the ground, about two inches apart. They were perfectly straight, and perfectly parallel. They stretched across the terrace, and Bishu stood at the far end.

'Come here,' he said. 'I'll show you how to walk like a man.'

Orko walked towards Bishu, more self-conscious than ever. His left foot felt heavier than his right, and the faster he tried to walk, the more off-balance he felt. Bishu had a look in his eyes that made Orko very uncomfortable. He felt as if his every move was being scrutinised – that he was being evaluated, and the prognosis wasn't good.

Bishu took him by the shoulders and turned him around. He stooped, placing Orko's left foot to the left of the lines, and his right foot to the right. 'Now, walk to the other end. Don't let your feet cross the lines,' he said.

Orko walked, slowly, awkwardly, to the other end of the terrace. It was harder than he had imagined. He was reminded of the time when his father bought him his first pair of jeans. After the first day of wearing them, his inner thighs were chafed, and they smarted when they brushed together. He had walked about awkwardly, with a sense of imbalance and sprawl, for days.

'There, wasn't that easy?' Bishu said with a smile.

Orko nodded, although he wasn't sure if he agreed.

'Do you have a terrace at home?' Bishu asked.

'Yes, sir, I do,' said Orko.

'Draw lines like these on your terrace. Practise walking every day, like you practise taking shots at the goal,' Bishu said. 'When you get the walk right, everything will fall into place.' He patted Orko on the back. 'And stop playing with Urmila, and all the other girls. Start behaving like a man and no one will dare bully you. You'll find that they're nice boys after all.'

Orko wanted to tell Bishu that the name was Urmi, but he didn't. It was very unlikely that Bishu and Urmi would ever meet.

On his way home, he imagined a pair of parallel lines drawn in blue tailor's chalk, all the way from Bishu's doorstep to his own. He walked slowly, deliberately, his feet straddling the imaginary lines. When he neared the football field, he began to feel silly walking like that. It would be really embarrassing if Urmi saw him. He ran, as fast as he could, until he reached home.

The blue lines drawn in tailor's chalk are everywhere now, a reminder of the fact that Orko isn't merely a boy who'd rather be a girl. He has a grave disease, and it makes boys hate him and call him names. It is the reason why no one takes him seriously. Finally, it all makes sense. It is as if he had these tiny pieces of a puzzle and they've suddenly come together to reveal a picture that fills Orko with despair.

In the beginning, Orko didn't want to believe that he had a disease. He was healthy, and he was reasonably intelligent. He did well in school, and he had friends that he liked being with. Before he went to that football camp, no one had ever told him he was sick. On the other hand, Bishu was a famous footballer, and he had shelves full of medals and trophies. He seemed to know what he was talking about. Orko couldn't dismiss Bishu's hypothesis, and it was proven when, one day, he showed up for a football game during his lunch break at school. The boys laughed at him. 'Go play hopscotch with the girls,' said Kaushik, and the boys laughed some more.

Orko slunk away to the guava tree behind the school buildings. He sat on the parapet, the world turning circles around him. 'I don't feel too well,' he said when his friends came looking for him. They asked him what was wrong, but Orko couldn't say. 'Let's all sit here today,' Nilanjana said, and they sat with him on the parapet, but Orko didn't hear a word they were saying. He wanted to cry but he couldn't. He looked around him. These were his friends, and they were all girls. Bishu was right. He was sick. He stood up and, as he walked away, Urmi called after him; Orko didn't stop, and he didn't look back.

Now, Orko is an island. At school, he still shares his tiffin with his friends, but he doesn't join them when they go for a walk afterwards. He barely speaks to his classmates, and his teachers often call him out for seeming distracted. His schoolwork isn't what it used to be, because he no longer does his homework with Urmi.

At the football camp he can't concentrate anymore, and Bishu seldom picks him for the team. He watches the game through the nylon netting strung between the goalposts, and feels as though he's in a cage. Sometimes, when he's really angry, he's outside the cage: the football game is a science experiment and the players are all mice, running after a ball of cheese.

After the game, Bishu takes him home, and although he's numb with dread, he quietly climbs onto the crossbar of Bishu's bicycle. On Bishu's terrace, he learns how to be a man. He knows now that he should be proud of his penis, and he shouldn't sit with his knees pressed together. He knows that he shouldn't carry his books clasped to his chest. Girls do that, because they don't want boys to gawk at their breasts. Girls are nothing. They don't have to be strong, because when they grow up, they'll be married and their husbands will look after them. They have to be pretty, to attract good husbands.

From the terrace, they go inside, to the bedroom. Orko is still too girly, and he must be punished. The room is grey. His body is grey, and it doesn't belong to him. There's coconut oil, but it does little for the piercing pain that he now knows intimately. He lies still, but that just adds to Bishu's rage. When the rage subsides, Bishu leaves the room, and comes back with a roshogolla, or a bar of chocolate. Orko's reward, for having endured the punishment like a man.

His life seems a charade now. It's exhausting to keep up this charade, because most of the time it seems futile. The boys at the football camp no longer tease him, but they aren't his friends. He can never be friends with them. Bishu has warned him that he mustn't tell anyone about the disease, and he can't talk to Urmi or Nilanjana because he's scared that he'll end up telling them everything. He's in a deep, dark hole, all alone, screaming a silent scream. The hole grows deeper every time he goes to Bishu's house, but he can't bring himself to stop going, because Bishu is his only hope. He knows that he isn't cured yet, because he still hates football, and he burns with envy at the sight of pretty earrings dangling from the earlobes of strangers.

Four

The tail-lights of the taxi recede into the distance. They flicker as the decrepit contraption slows to a halt near the mouth of the lane. Four quick flashes of yellow and it's gone, leaving behind only a whiff of burnt diesel in the air.

The one-legged signpost maintains its solitary vigil by the entrance. Orko pushes the gate open; it's so quiet that he can hear flakes of rust coming off the hinges. The cluster of flats is a patchwork of dark and light – fluorescent white, incandescent yellow, shadowy grey. A cricket chirps in the distance.

The stairwell is dark, but Orko knows each of the forty-two steps, each crack in the concrete banister. He can't see the nameplate on the door as he feels his way around the padlock. The key turns with a click. He quietly slips off the padlock, but when he undoes the deadbolt it clatters against the door panel. He closes the door behind him, quietly, as if he were an intruder in his own home. When he switches on the light, the sight of his hand on the switch is strange and unfamiliar.

'Hello,' he says to no one, because tonight he's alone. 'Hello,' he says again, and again, varying the pitch of his voice, but it still doesn't sound right.

This night of being alone came about suddenly. He fretted about the board examinations as he meandered through Fern Road after school. On the bus, he revisited the practice test they were given, and he knew immediately that he had done poorly. When he was at the mouth of the lane, the thought of the stack of melamine bowls in the fridge killed his appetite. At the front door, he fished out his keys from his pocket but the padlock was gone. Confused, he rang the bell.

'I have to leave for Hazaribagh tonight,' Nandan said as he opened the door. 'Kabul-kaka has had a heart attack.'

Kabul is Orko's great-uncle; Orko calls him Kabul-dadu. He's a doctor, and he once worked for the government of Bihar. Orko doesn't remember the specifics of how they're related – only that Kabul-dadu was born in Kabul. He's a little embarrassed by this, because when they were on the train to Hazaribagh a few years ago, his father drew their family tree on a scrap of paper and marked the relevant branches. As the train pulled into the station, Nandan was at the door, restless, searching for a face in the crowd on the platform. 'Tenia!' he called out, his face alight with a boyish smile that Orko had never seen before. He waved, and a man in the crowd waved back. The man ran alongside the train, boarding their compartment even before the train had come to a halt. Orko was surprised when Nandan embraced the man, because he had never seen his father embrace anyone.

'This is Tenia-kaka,' Nandan said. 'We've been friends for the longest time.'

'The last time I saw you, you were a little baby,' the man said to Orko.

They drove for what seemed like hours, until they came to a tall gate set in a boundary wall that looked like a giant mouse had nibbled off portions of it. Kabul-dadu was at the gate when they arrived. He looked older than Orko's father, but not quite as old as his grandfather. He lived by himself in a house that was the largest Orko had ever seen, and it looked like it was hundreds of years old. Much of the house was closed off – windows were nailed shut, doors boarded over, and across their frames were cobwebs that looked like they had hung there for decades. Kabul-dadu told Orko that the house had once been a palace. The stables had been converted into a garage, and by the stables was a small outhouse. Tenia lived there, with his daughter, Lali.

Lali was a few years older than Orko. The first hour they spent together was awkward, because Lali's Bangla wasn't very good, and Orko had just started Hindi lessons at school. Before the day was over, though, they were playing together by the defunct fountain in the garden. They pretended that the headless cherub at its centre was a castle, and the pool around it was a moat. Tenia's goat had recently given birth to a kid, and the tiny creature was a dragon that liked to set things on fire.

'What's a dragon?' Lali asked him.

'It's a giant flying creature. It breathes fire, and it eats up everyone in sight,' said Orko.

Lali laughed, and Orko thought it was because of his poor Hindi.

'There's no such thing,' she said.

The kid kept trying to climb out of the fountain. It bleated frantically when it lost its footing. After a while, Lali gathered it up in her arms and took it back to its mother.

Now, Lali is a mother, and she no longer lives in the outhouse by the stables. Kabul-dadu is gravely ill, and Orko's father is on his way to the house that had once been a palace. Orko is home alone, and this flat in which he has lived all his life seems strange and unfamiliar.

He can't fathom why he feels this way. Everything is where it should be. The dining table is in the corner, by the kitchen door, with the three mismatched chairs around it. The sofa set is exactly where it has been for as long as he can remember. The calendar on the wall shows November, with the jagged edge of October still showing near the crimp. The refrigerator is by the door to his room, with his mother's photograph on it, just like it had been in the morning.

In the picture, his mother's cheeks are less filled out than he remembers. She's looking at him, mildly amused, and not for the first time Orko is annoyed with her. The last words she wrote to him are inscribed on the title page of an abridged version of *Moby-Dick*. 'Dearest Orko,' she wrote, 'this is one of my favourite stories. You must read the grown-up version when you're older.' She had bought the book for his eighth birthday, but it was his grandfather who handed it to him, after he came home from the hospital. He didn't read much into the inscription at the time, but now it seems that she knew she wouldn't be around when he was old enough to read the unabridged *Moby-Dick*. He wishes he could tell her that he loved the story too, but the truth is that every time he reads the book, it seems a little more revolting.

In Orko's wardrobe, hidden behind his winter clothes, is the old cardboard box with his mother's notebooks. When they came into his possession, he couldn't imagine that he would read them one day. Tonight, he pushes aside the stack of sweaters and scarves and cradles the box in his arms. It smells of mothballs.

There are seven notebooks in all. He lays them out on his bed. When he was little, he often played with his mother's things, and she always knew exactly what he had been up to. Now, of course, he isn't little anymore, and he's much better at keeping secrets.

One of the notebooks is emerald-green and larger than the others. On the first page is his mother's maiden name and a date. His mother was seventeen when she started this notebook. At twenty, she was married, and she no longer went by the name inscribed on this page. Near the centre of the page, in large block letters, is the word 'PRIVATE'.

Orko dwells on the meaning of that word, and he decides that it means entirely different things to different people. Urmi marked her diaries that way when they were young children, but she often let him read them anyway. In her notebooks she wrote stories, inspired by the Famous Five. She would change the names of the characters to Bodhi, Urmi and Orko, but when he read the stories he knew Orko was really George, because in the Famous Five stories, George was a girl who dressed like a boy.

The notebook has no margins or lines. It starts with a pencil sketch of a butterfly, with stripes like a zebra's. There are a few pages of song lyrics in English and in Bangla, interspersed with sketches of a young girl. In one of the sketches, she's looking straight into his eyes, and Orko is a little rattled because she looks like she could be his sister. In another, she's looking away. She's naked, and her left shoulder is obscured by a butterfly's wing.

The next notebook is smaller, and thicker. The cover is nondescript, and the first page doesn't have any markings on it. The sketches are fewer, in blue ink. The writing is dense;

the colour of the ink changes from page to page. In the first few pages, his mother is exasperated because her father won't let her go to Shantiniketan to study fine arts. She rants, and she writes terrible poems about birds in cages. About halfway through the notebook her father relents, and she writes that she always knew he would. Orko is confused, because as far as he knows, his mother never went to Shantiniketan to study fine arts. He becomes distracted and flips through the rest of the pages, but there are just sketches with illegible scribbles near the margins.

In the notebook dated two years before his birth, his mother does, in fact, go to Shantiniketan. Orko feels a little unhinged, because all his life he has been given to believe that his mother studied English literature, and that she graduated from a college in the city, two years after he was born. On the page before him, the ink is black. His mother is overwhelmed by her august surroundings, and she's in awe of her brilliant classmates. She worries that she's an impostor, and that she's never going to be any good. When her despair is at its worst, a man appears, in green ink. His name is Indrajit, and at first his mother finds him annoying. She complains that he smells of cheap cigarettes, and that he writes pretentious poetry about poverty and about revolution, while making it known that he comes from a family of means. He plays the guitar and sings folk songs in Bangla, but he secretly listens to opera. A few pages later, she worries that her father won't like Indrajit, and she contemplates running away with him to the badlands of Bihar. The notebook ends there, and Orko feverishly opens the next one. On the first page is his mother's married name. The rest of the notebook is empty.

Orko lies in bed with the stack of notebooks by his side. Through his childhood, he had always known that he wanted to be like his mother, and now, alone in this flat that she once inhabited, he realises that when she was a young girl, she was much like he is now. She daydreamed, like him, and she wrote down song lyrics in her notebooks. Like him, she didn't understand why she wanted the things that she did. She was wracked by self-doubt and, like him, felt like an impostor among her peers.

He remembers how she laughed until she was out of breath, and he laughed with her, even when he didn't know why she was laughing. He remembers her, in the kitchen, smoking a cigarette. When she saw him at the door, she quickly threw the cigarette out of the window, and her manner was much like his own when she caught him playing with her lipstick. She wiped her face with her saree, but Orko knew she had been crying. He has never seen his father cry, or laugh until he was short of breath and there were tears at the corners of his eyes.

Outside, the night is nearly gone. The sky is a greyish pink, and Orko wishes he didn't have to go to school in a few hours.

In Orko's father's bedroom are two identical steel wardrobes, side by side. The one on the right belongs to his father; a bunch of keys hangs from the keyhole. It's a beautiful silver keyring, with an ornamental clasp. The wardrobe on the left is his mother's; it hasn't been opened in years. Orko can picture his mother standing right here, in front of the mirror, as she wrapped her saree around her. He watched her countless times, enthralled by her intricate, fluid movements as she put on her saree. The wrap, the pleat, the tuck and the drape. It was a dance, and at the end of this dance she looked at herself in the mirror, sideways, as she clipped the silver keyring at her waist. It hung there, by his cheek, when he wrapped his arms around her. The saree was moss-green, and she smelt of lavender.

It was winter then. His mother was in the kitchen, and Orko was by himself, in front of this very mirror. He pretended that his mother's shawl was a saree. He fumbled through the steps – the wrap, the pleat, the tuck, the drape. The pleats came out wrong, because the shawl was too thick, too wide and not nearly long enough. As he ran to the kitchen, his saree unravelled behind him.

'Show me how to wear it,' he said to his mother.

That was when she told him that sarees were for girls, and he wasn't a girl.

'How do you know that I'm not a girl?' he asked her.

'I'm your mother,' she replied. 'I know everything.'

'But how do you know?' he persisted.

'Because you have a penis,' she said as she threw a handful of something into the frying pan. It crackled and sputtered, and the kitchen was filled with a pungent smoke that stung his eyes.

'You mean girls don't have penises?' he asked her, alarmed, his hand inside his shorts.

'No, they don't,' she said, stirring the thing that was in the frying pan.

'How do they pee then?' he asked.

'They have a little opening, right where your penis is.'

Orko thought about that for a while. He still remembers the moment when it became clear as day. 'So if I didn't have a penis, I could do whatever I want?'

'That's not entirely true,' his mother said. The pressure cooker let out a terrifying hiss, and Orko waited patiently for his mother to finish whatever she was doing to it. He felt desperate.

'What if we went to the doctor and asked him to cut it off?' he asked. 'Can I wear a saree then? And earrings, like Urmi?'

'You can't just cut off parts of your body,' his mother said. 'Each part of your body is there for a reason.'

'But you don't have a penis, and you're okay,' he said.

'There are things that you won't understand until you're grown up,' his mother replied.

Orko walked back to his mother's room, crestfallen. He remembers that he left the shawl on the kitchen floor, because he got a scolding afterwards. It wasn't very long after this that his mother disappeared. Everybody said she died because her heart stopped beating; Orko didn't believe it then, and he only half-believes it now.

His mother's wardrobe is an everyday piece of furniture. There's one like it in almost every bedroom that he has been in. The taupe paint has begun to peel near the edges. There's an arc around the keyhole, flecked with rust, where the keys scraped the paint when his mother left them hanging there. There's a full-length mirror on the left panel. He removes the keys from his father's wardrobe and holds them up by the clasp. He selects a key at random and inserts it into the keyhole of his mother's wardrobe. When it turns all the way, he's breathless.

He gently pushes the handle downwards. It lets out a screech of protest. He tugs at the handle, and the door comes ajar with a dull metallic whine as the hinges grate against the rust of the years. The lower shelves are empty, lined with yellowing newspaper from a decade ago. Above them, level with his eyes, are his mother's dress sarees – she wore these to weddings and to dinner invitations. She would be very cross if he took one of these.

He gingerly touches the blue silk saree in the far right corner. It's smoother than it looks, and it's cold to the touch. This is a special saree; his mother wore it two days after her wedding, for a ceremony that required her to serve food to her new husband's family. The saree looks fragile, and he moves on to another one. This one is peach, with a black border. It's stiff with starch. He carefully takes it off its hanger and spreads it out on the bed, like his mother used to. The folds are stubborn, like the folds of a letter that was forgotten for decades between the pages of a book. He tucks the top edge of the diaphanous garment into the waistband of his jeans. He surprises himself by the dexterity with which he brings it together – the wrap, the pleat, the tuck. As he's draping the trail over his shoulder, he realises that he's worn it the wrong way around; his mother always had the drape over her right shoulder. He unwinds it, all the way. He wants it to be just right, and wearing a saree over a pair of jeans and a T-shirt doesn't feel right.

On the top shelf is a stack of blouses and petticoats, but he can't find a set that goes with the saree. He picks a different saree – the mauve one that his mother wore when she went to visit Urmi's mother, or to the grocery shops in the neighbourhood. He takes off his shirt. There's a wispy growth of hair on his chest, and he tries not to look at it as he puts on the blouse. It's a little tight around his shoulders as he fastens the hooks. He steps out of his jeans and into the mauve petticoat. When he's done fastening the drawstring around his waist, the garment falls an inch short of his ankles. He tucks the edge of the saree into the waistband, and he winds it the right way this time. This saree is lighter, and it isn't starched.

He's almost pleased by what he sees in the mirror. His hair is too short, his earlobes are bare and his chest is as flat as a board, but the saree looks pretty on him. He whirls around and around, until the room is turning circles around him. He looks at his reflection, sideways, like his mother used to when she dressed for a special occasion. He clips the keyring to his waistband and paces the floor, as if he's trying on a new pair of shoes.

He has never felt like this before. He loves the sensation of the soft fabric against his skin. He feels unfettered, his legs unconstrained. He pictures himself walking down the Gariahat boulevard with Urmi. The tables are turned now – she's the child, in her school uniform, and he's the grown-up, in a saree. He feels afloat, like a feather in the breeze.

When he glances at the mirror again, he remembers a tram ride with his father a few years ago. A woman boarded their carriage, in a saree much like the one he's wearing now. She had a well-worn handbag on her shoulder, and a large jute shopping bag in her hand. Some of the men in the carriage started heckling her, and when she protested, the pitch of her voice was lower than the average woman's. The conductor refused to sound the bell until she left the carriage.

'Who was that woman?' Orko had asked his father when they got off the tram. 'Why did they treat her like that?'

'That's no woman,' said his father. 'He's a hijra. A damaged man. They shouldn't have treated him so badly, though.'

'Why didn't you say something, then?' he asked.

'When you live in society, you agree to follow a set of rules,' said his father. 'When you break the rules, you have to be prepared for the consequences.'

'But she wasn't bothering anyone,' Orko protested.

'Well, if he dressed like a decent man, no one would bother him,' his father replied.

To Orko, the woman in the tram didn't look like a man at all. Nothing about her manner was masculine in any way. He imagined her in trousers and a polo shirt, like his father was wearing that day, but it didn't quite fit.

Since that tram ride, Orko has come across many more hijra people. Although his father said that they were men, this is difficult for Orko to accept. It is true that some of them are more manly than others, but it seems inaccurate to refer to them as men. They don't dress like men. They don't talk or walk like men, with that air of entitlement about them. When they speak among themselves, there is a distinct incongruity between the timbre of their voices and the inflections at the end of their sentences. They don't work in offices and in banks; they aren't shop minders or bus conductors or rickshaw drivers. They are on the footpath, milling around food stalls, clapping, until the vendor pays them or gives them some free food to make them go away. They are at traffic signals, clapping at car windows until disembodied hands appear through hastily rolled down windows to drop a few coins in their outstretched palms.

Last Tuesday, Orko was going to Bishu's house, riding on the crossbar of Bishu's bicycle, when they passed a troupe of hijras, singing and dancing in front of a one-storey house.

The youngest of them couldn't have been much older than Orko. She was wearing a yellow saree, and her golden earrings shone in the sun. Her long black hair was in a bun, held together with a pencil. Her features held the faintest of clues that she had once been a boy.

She smiled at them when they passed, and this made Bishu very angry. He let loose a string of expletives, many of which Orko had never heard before. When they had left the hijras behind, he told Orko that they carried off babies and young boys and chopped off their penises with a machete. The boys' families were so ashamed that they didn't even file a police report. The boys with the severed penises remained with the hijras, and that was how they grew their number.

'But why do they do that?' Orko asked, incredulous.

'Because they themselves are damaged. They're perverts. Deviants. And let me tell you this – if you don't change your ways, they're going to come after you.'

Although a part of him was horrified, Orko couldn't help but wonder about the girl in the yellow saree. She was like any other young girl, and she didn't look like she was being held against her will.

When they went upstairs, to the room on the terrace, Bishu was still angry. 'I saw the way you looked at that young one,' he said. 'You're one of them, aren't you?'

When Bishu asked him to take off his clothes, he complied swiftly. Bishu's gaze followed him as he hurried to the bed. He lay face-down, and imagined that he was alone in this room, with no one leering at him. The sheet smelt of mildew, its block print a maroon blur. He bit his lip as Bishu moved inside of him. It went on forever and, near the end, all sensation ceased. It was almost as if he were floating above the bed, watching Bishu's corpulent form writhe against the body of a stranger. He came crashing down when the familiar grunt escaped Bishu's throat. He hoped Bishu wouldn't ask him to do the other thing, and he realised, in that moment, that Bishu had his own designs on him, and the lessons were just a pretext. He no longer believed a word Bishu said. The hijras couldn't possibly be so cruel as to chop off penises with machetes. He didn't see that depravity in their eyes. Bishu was the depraved one. Bishu was the pervert.

Now, Orko is angrier than he has ever been. He's angry with Bishu, of course. He's angry with his father for suggesting that he join the football camp. Most of all, he's angry with himself for putting up with it for so long.

It's three in the afternoon, and although Orko hasn't eaten all day, he isn't hungry. When the phone rings he knows it's his father even before he picks up the receiver.

'I'm going to be here for a few more days,' his father says. 'Kabul-kaka is better, but he isn't out of the woods yet.'

'Okay,' says Orko. When his voice broke a few years ago, Orko was deeply unsettled. It took him a while to grow used to the gruff, uneven sound, and during those months he spoke only when it was absolutely necessary. Now his voice sounds strange again, and suddenly he doesn't feel pretty anymore.

'I've spoken to your aunt,' his father goes on. 'She's expecting you. You're to stay with her until I'm back.'

'Okay,' says Orko again. He sits there by the phone, wishing that he didn't have to go to his aunt's house. He wishes he could be here, by himself, forever. He wishes he could go to Urmi's, in the saree, and sit at her kitchen table, sharing a pot of tea with her. He thinks about the girl in the yellow saree, and it dawns on him that he doesn't know her name.

Five

It's evening when Orko reaches his grandfather's house. Sudeshna suggests they have dinner at a Chinese restaurant in the neighbourhood. 'It's a new restaurant,' she says. 'Manju's family runs the place.'

The name doesn't ring a bell, and Orko isn't particularly keen on having a conversation with a stranger. When they reach the restaurant, which is called the Golden Dragon, his aunt asks after Manju even before they're seated. Orko is relieved when the doorman informs them that she won't be coming in tonight.

They're the only diners at the restaurant. They choose a table in the corner, away from the air conditioner. There's a menu card on their table. Sudeshna slides it across to Orko, but he hands it back to her without reading it. 'I'll just have some soup,' he says. Sudeshna orders chicken soup, with sweet corn. Orko tells the waiter that they're cold. The man hurries away with an inscrutable nod of his head.

The Golden Dragon is, in many ways, a typical Chinese restaurant. There are six tables in all, draped in chequered tablecloths, red and white. At the centre of their table are three glass pods, containing soya sauce, chilli sauce and chopped green chillies floating in vinegar. The music is typical, and although he hasn't heard this particular tune, he knows that it's Kenny G. Their waiter stands by the entrance to the kitchen, and he refills Sudeshna's glass moments after she takes a sip of water. Orko imagines having a job like that, standing by the kitchen door for hours, keeping track of every sip of water, every mouthful of chow mein.

The dim lighting reminds him of the room on Bishu's terrace. He counts the squares on the tablecloth to distract himself, but he can't get to twenty before he has to start over. He hears his aunt speak, but he doesn't comprehend the words. The inflection at the end of the sentence tells him that it had been a question. He can't stop counting the squares on the tablecloth. He's up to sixty-seven when she reaches for his hand.

'Is everything all right, Orko?' she asks.

'I'm just a little tired,' Orko replies. He tries to smile, but his eyes well up with tears. The glass pods shimmer against the red and white squares.

'I've known you since the day you were born,' says his aunt. 'You're going to have to do better than that.'

Orko considers making up a story, but he knows, from years of experience, that he won't get away with it.

'Baba sent me to a football camp,' he begins. The rest of it comes to him in a series of stills, like a story about somebody else. He tries to make a simple sentence, to describe the images, but he can't. He remembers the time when he was convinced that his father was mixed up with terrorists – he had been absolutely sanguine, and yet, when he started putting the pieces together so his grandfather would understand, it all fell apart. And then his grandfather died.

He draws a deep breath, but it is as if all the oxygen has been sucked out of the room. There's something straining against the insides of his chest, and the moment he becomes aware of it, it rushes out of him in a wretched whimper.

His aunt is by his side in the blink of an eye. She puts her arm around him. The waiter rushes to their table, but his aunt waves him away. She places her hand between his shoulder blades and he feels the air rush into his lungs. He begins to shiver, and he knows that he can't hold back anymore. He weeps, until his head hurts and his cheeks are muddy with tears. The tip of his nose feels numb. He reaches for a napkin, but it is crisp to the touch. His aunt offers him the trail of her saree. He remembers blowing his nose on this saree, but he can't remember if it was his mother or his aunt who was wearing it at the time.

They sit quietly, side by side, until the waiter brings them their soup. It smells delicious, and Orko remembers that he hasn't eaten all day. He wolfs down the steaming bowl of soup in silence. His aunt takes her time, and Orko is glad, because Sudeshna speaks very little while she's eating.

'Would you like some chow mein?' she asks him as she tilts the bowl away from her for the last spoonful of soup. He shakes his head, and his aunt asks their waiter for the bill. Orko resumes his count of the squares on the tablecloth, ashamed that he made such a spectacle of himself.

The waiter returns with the change. Sudeshna leaves behind a few coins, fewer than his father leaves as a tip when they eat at the Chinese restaurant in their neighbourhood. The man at the door smiles at them, but Orko looks away. On the short walk back to his grandfather's house, he walks a few steps ahead of his aunt. He's afraid that he's going to end up telling her about the room on Bishu's terrace, and that she won't want anything to do with him afterwards. When they're back in the house, he heads straight for the bathroom, and he stays there for much longer than it takes him to brush his teeth and change into his pyjamas.

The last time he spent the night in this house, Orko was in his grandfather's room, and he slept poorly, if at all. There was a presence in the room that night, and he felt as if he were being watched. He switched on the light but the feeling refused to go away. He doesn't believe in ghosts anymore, but that night he had wished he wasn't alone.

When he comes out of the bathroom, his mouth smelling of toothpaste, his aunt is in bed, reading. 'May I sleep in your room tonight?' he asks her sheepishly.

His aunt looks up from her book. 'Of course you can,' she says. Orko feels like he's twelve years old again, because that's how old he was the last time he slept in his aunt's bed. She ruffles his hair. 'Good boy,' she says, before she turns out the light.

Orko lies in bed stiffly, his hands on his stomach. He feels distinctly odd, lying beside his aunt in the dark. He worries that he's going to kick her in his sleep. Outside, the sounds of traffic die out as the evening winds down. His aunt's silhouette is perfectly still, and it reminds Orko of his grandfather's lifeless form in the armchair on the balcony. He listens for the sound of her breathing, but all he can hear is the ticking of the clock on the nightstand. Just as he's beginning to panic, she raises her hand to her mouth and lets out a quiet cough.

'You don't have to go to the football camp if you don't want to,' she says.

'Baba said that I should play a team sport,' he replies. While that isn't a lie, it isn't the truth either. The truth is that he signed up for football to spite Urmi, and he continues to go to Bishu's terrace because he's afraid that he is going to be expelled, and that she will laugh at him if she finds out.

'I've spent ten years teaching adolescent boys,' Sudeshna says ruefully. 'I wish you asked me before you signed up.' Orko hears her sigh over the ticking of the clock on the night-stand. 'I don't know what happened to you, but something clearly has,' she continues. 'I just want you to know that you're a beautiful boy. Sometimes people will treat you badly, for no reason at all. You must always remember that it's not your fault.'

Not for the first time this week, Orko feels like an impostor. Just this morning, as he spoke to his father on the phone while dressed in his mother's saree, he felt like the ugliest creature alive. Even the kindest person in the whole world wouldn't say that he was beautiful. Would his aunt still think that he was beautiful and blameless if she saw him dressed like that?

Orko never was a brilliant student. Sometimes he feels incredibly fortunate for having come this far without a stumble. He has always paid attention in class, and a few hours of study before the annual examinations have been enough to see him through. This year, though, his luck seems to have run out. The texts seem incredibly dense, and his notes are so erratic that they're completely useless. He's more than a little unnerved as he reads through the pages from less than a week ago. Therefore, say the three terse dots stacked in a pyramid, the left-hand side of the equation equals the right. It ought to make sense, but it doesn't.

He's sure that everyone else in his class is better prepared than he is. They seem to have a sense of purpose. Most of them have already decided that they're going to study science after their board examinations. He, on the other hand, hasn't been able to make up his mind. His father is of the opinion that he should study humanities, and Orko can't help thinking that this is because his father thinks he's stupid. Bodhi, Urmi's brother, is studying to be an engineer at an elite institute in Kanpur. In Bodhi's higher secondary class, all the boys were in the science section. In the humanities section there were seven girls – and, according to Bodhi, they were all dolts. They were studying humanities only because they weren't offered science, and it didn't matter, because they were just killing time in the school system, preparing themselves for the marriage market.

Orko didn't agree with Bodhi's assertion. Nilanjana wanted to study fine arts, and Bodhi's own sister wanted to study history. They certainly weren't idiots, and he had never heard them speak about getting married. He'd said nothing to Bodhi at the time, because he was sure Bodhi would put him down with a clever remark, and he would feel extremely stupid for having spoken his mind.

He pores over the scribbled minutiae in the pages of his notebook. This is his third pass this morning, but it still doesn't make any sense. Years ago, he sat at this very table, his aunt by his side. She was teaching him that the angles of a triangle added up to a hundred and eighty degrees, and he remembers the ease with which she went about proving it. He can hear her in the kitchen now, filling a vessel from the faucet – a kettle, by the sound of it. He leaves his books on the dining table and sidles up to her.

'Are you making tea?' he asks.

'Yes, I am,' she says. 'Would you like some?'

'Yes, please,' Orko replies.

Although Orko has always lived with his father, he has often thought of Sudeshna as his guardian – the grown-up who saw to his homework and bought him new clothes before the pujo. When he was in her charge, he was often infuriated by the fact that nothing seemed to escape her notice. Now, she's alone, with no one to take care of, and he wonders how her life might have turned out if the twin catastrophes of her sister's death and her father's illness hadn't brought her back to Calcutta. She used to be the head of the biology department at an elite school in Dehradun. His father once told him that her students were terrified of her, and Orko remembers wondering how his father knew this.

If Sudeshna hadn't come back to Calcutta, Nandan would probably have moved back to his parents' home in Hazra. Orko would live there too, with Robi and Ria, taking the school bus home, eating his meals quietly, efficiently, like a food digestion device – charm, chew, masticate, swallow. In a few years, he would be expected to be an active participant in the stultifying conversations about cricket and politics when they sat down to tea. He would probably have to share Robi's room, and that would be horrible, because Robi's taste in music is appalling, and after he has been to the toilet there's always a few drops of piss on the seat.

They bring their tea to the dining table in the hall adjoining the kitchen. Of the six windows, just one is open.

Outside, it is almost noon; in the room, the light is soft and golden, like sunset in winter.

Sudeshna heads back into the kitchen and returns with a biscuit tin. This tin is in Orko's earliest memories. He remembers his mother, at the coffee table on the balcony, struggling to prise the lid open. Sudeshna opens the lid effortlessly and sets it down by Orko's teacup. This was his grandfather's place at the table. Time warps, and he's ten again. His grandfather's enamelled bowl; the brass tumbler in the shape of a tulip by its side; the pale green napkin that Sudeshna tucked into his grandfather's collar when they sat down to lunch.

'You're having trouble with your studies,' his aunt says, just as the clock finishes announcing that it is now noon. Her tone is neutral, and Orko isn't surprised that she knows. He has been sitting at the dining table all morning, flitting between his mathematics textbook and his sketchy notes. 'I know,' he says. 'I'm trying my best, but none of it is making sense.' He's surprised, because he has never admitted this – even to himself.

Sudeshna places her palms on the table, side by side. She draws them apart, as if smoothing over the creases in an imaginary tablecloth. Orko follows the tips of her fingers as she lifts her hands off the table and clasps them together.

'You remind me of your mother,' she says. 'You're so much like her that it's uncanny.'

Orko is taken completely by surprise. His aunt hasn't spoken of his mother in years.

'What do you mean?' he asks.

'She was brilliant,' she says. 'But something came over her just before her matriculation exams. She would sit here, at this table, her books open in front of her, and I could tell that she was struggling. I tried to help, but it was as if she didn't hear me, or see me, or comprehend a word I said.'

Orko can't imagine that his mother ever struggled with her studies. She was the one with all the answers. She could never be as lost as he feels now. 'I'm not brilliant,' he retorts.

'You are,' his aunt says. 'You're just like her, and I'm afraid for you.'

A strange emotion takes hold of Orko. It's almost like happiness, but there's an edge to it, and it cuts him, like the edge of a page of a new book. He lifts his teacup with both hands and brings it to his lips. The teacup is warm and he cups his hands around it.

His aunt watches him with a look of mild amusement. 'Each time I tell myself that I'm imagining things, you go and do something like that,' she says. She has a faraway look in her eyes. 'A spitting image,' she says under her breath. She sets her cup down, and it strikes the saucer with a hollow metallic clink.

'When she was your age, she began to grow apart from her friends.' Sudeshna stares at the surface of the table as if the story of his mother's life were inscribed upon it. 'She spent hours by herself, scribbling in her notebooks. Once, we were having dinner, right here, at this table, and she looked completely out of it. Baba asked her if everything was all right, and she burst into tears. She cried until she was gasping for breath, just like you were yesterday.'

Sudeshna looks at Orko again, and he feels a little unnerved. He feels as if she's analysing him, picking apart every action, every mannerism.

She fidgets with the end of her saree. 'I still don't know what the matter was,' she says ruefully. 'In fact, it was around that time that she stopped confiding in me. She spoke only when spoken to. This went on for months, and then she ran away from home.'

Sudeshna glances at Orko fleetingly, and he knows that he appears less surprised than he should be – his mother had devoted several pages in her notebooks to her elaborate plans to run away. He himself has considered it, but he could never muster the courage.

'Where did she go?' he asks.

'I don't know. She wouldn't say.' Sudeshna looks like she's trying to remember something that happened many years ago. 'She wanted to grow up in a hurry,' she continues. 'When she was twelve or thirteen, I had just started college. She would dress up in my sarees, my earrings. She would spend hours at my dressing table, trying on different shades of lipstick. She would read my books, and when she spoke to my friends you wouldn't imagine that she was six years younger than me.'

Orko tries to picture his mother as a young girl, trying on her big sister's clothes. Instead, he sees himself at his aunt's dressing table, in the mauve saree he took from his mother's wardrobe. He's so embarrassed that he closes his eyes.

Sudeshna takes his hand in hers. 'When she was pregnant with you, she was sure you were going to be a girl. She was going to call you Orkopriya. She used to say that she would give you all the things that she couldn't have.'

'Orkopriya...' Without meaning to, he says the name aloud. He likes the sound of it.

'You were a beautiful baby. For the first few years it didn't even register that you're a boy. She would dress you in the pinafores she wore as a toddler. Sometimes she put a flower in your hair when she took you out for a stroll. She absolutely adored you, and that's why, I'm afraid—'

'Afraid?' Orko asks tentatively.

'—that she hasn't been able to let go of you.'

Sudeshna looks distraught, and Orko is a little unnerved. He has never seen his aunt lose her composure.

'What do you mean?' he asks, but she goes on as if she hasn't heard him.

'When you were twelve, I saw you at my dressing table. You were wearing maroon lipstick, and you looked just like her. That's when I began to suspect that your mother's spirit is still with you.'

Strangely enough, Orko isn't embarrassed about the fact that his aunt saw him wearing her lipstick. He wants to tell her that his mother's spirit was not to blame; he did that even when his mother was alive. The first time his mother caught him with streaks of burgundy lipstick around his lips, she sent him to the balcony behind their kitchen, where he sat, quietly, for a period of time that seemed unbearably long, worrying that she was never going to talk to him again. He was relieved when she called for him from the kitchen. She told him that lipstick was for grown-ups, and he mustn't play with her lipstick again.

On the wall, a few feet to the left of the kitchen door, is a photograph of Orko's grandmother with her two daughters. In the photograph Sudeshna is a young girl, and his mother is an infant in her mother's arms.

'I told your father to go to Gaya, with her ashes, to set her free,' Sudeshna says, her gaze fixed on the photograph. 'I even offered to do it myself, but he wouldn't let me. He said it's all superstition, and that there's no such thing as a soul.'

She looks like she might begin to cry. Orko reaches for her hand, but she draws back and brings the drape of her saree to her face.

It is difficult for Orko to imagine his mother as a disembodied soul, trapped in an urn of ashes. He looks away, at the pendulum of the clock on the wall. He wills it to stop swinging for just a moment, but it's relentless, its ticking louder than he can bear. He doesn't know what he believes anymore.

'How did she die?' he asks his aunt. 'What happened to her?'

'Cardiac arrest,' his aunt replies.

He has heard this answer before, and he doesn't believe it any more than he did the first time he heard it. A twenty-nine year old heart doesn't just stop beating.

They sit there, for the longest time, in a silence punctuated by the ticking of the pendulum clock. The clock has hung above the kitchen door for as long as Orko can remember, and he has never paid it any mind. Now it seems alive, an active member of the household. The rhythm of its pendulum drives him to distraction.

'I think I'll go for a walk,' he says.

'Yes, you do that,' his aunt replies. 'When you're back, we'll work on this together.' She gestures at the books strewn on the table. She appears calm and composed now. She begins to clear away their empty teacups, and Orko wonders if he imagined their entire conversation.

'You're going to do very well,' Sudeshna says in parting. 'Your mother stood first in her class.'

Outside, the sun is a feeble glow obscured by a mass of clouds that looks like it has been painted onto the sky. Cars honk impatiently at no one in particular. A man and a woman pass Orko, the man's arm around the woman's waist. They walk at a leisurely pace, and Orko follows them listlessly, dragging his feet. The woman looks over her shoulder. Their glances meet, and Orko feels acutely embarrassed.

He prepares to cross the street, but the wall of vehicles seems impregnable. He waits impatiently for a lull in the traffic. Bumpers collide, and an altercation ensues. Orko ambles across to the footpath that skirts the lake. He climbs over the waist-high fence and lands softly on the yellowing grass. He can't see anybody else on the grounds. The horns from the cars on the street grow distant. He walks aimlessly along the shore. He passes a few benches until he comes to the one beneath the gulmohur. The bench is squat, backless, its concrete surface pockmarked with little craters, the brickwork showing through the deepest of them. Surprisingly, the bench is warm.

He lies on his back, beneath the dull grey sky. A sparrow flashes across his field of vision. He can hear crows in the tree behind the bench. Two, maybe three. They talk, back and forth, over each other, and then they fly away, beating their raven wings against the grey afternoon.

In all these years, Orko didn't really believe that his mother was dead. It didn't seem plausible, and there were too many holes in the story that he had pieced together from everything he was allowed to know. Two nights ago, as he read her notebooks, he became convinced that she was alive. Perhaps she was living with Indrajit in the badlands of Bihar; perhaps she was a schoolteacher, like his aunt used to be, living by herself in a sleepy town on a high mountain. Perhaps she was going to come back for him one day, when the things that drove her away were in the distant past. Of course, all of that had just been conjecture – wishful thinking, even. In contrast, Sudeshna's anguish was so real that he could almost reach out and touch it.

That anguish hangs about him, like a foul smog, and he finally begins to accept that his mother is dead. She really is gone. She isn't coming back for him. For a moment, he feels as if the wind has been knocked out of him, and when the moment passes he's finally able to picture his mother's body laid out on a rough-hewn bier, her ears and her nostrils closed off with cottonwool. He wonders if there is an essence of her that has existed from the beginning of time, and continues to exist, even after her body was consumed by the giant oven at the crematorium. Was it possible that his mother was wafting about in the ether, watching over him? Was she disappointed that he was not Orkopriya?

His thoughts scatter, disjointed, incongruent, devoid of meaning. Orko imagines himself against the grey sky, spiralling downwards like a bird of prey. There is a mutilated body laid out on the pockmarked bench, its face ripped away, its limbs laid out like the limbs of a discarded rag doll. The body is dressed in the clothes he is wearing now, but it is not him.

Six

It's almost eleven in the morning when the doorbell rings. Orko knows that it's his father. He continues to sit at the dining table, pretending to study.

'Orko!' his aunt calls out. She is in the bathroom, by the sound of it. 'Will you get the door, please?'

Orko shuffles to the door reluctantly. When he came to stay with his aunt a week ago, he wasn't really looking forward to it; everything in this house still reminded him of his grandfather. Over the past week, though, he has thought about his grandfather only fleetingly, and he has discovered how it feels to have a conversation with a grown-up who laughs, and cries, and becomes angry or regretful about things over which they never had any control. Besides, for the first time this year, he feels confident about the board examinations. He has a set routine, and his aunt is an excellent teacher. He has learnt more in a week than he did in the entire school year.

'How have you been?' Nandan asks as he comes through the door. 'I'm sorry I had to stay away for longer than I planned.'

'That's okay,' says Orko. 'How is Kabul-dadu?' he asks, even though his father told him over the phone that he's better now.

'He has been discharged from the hospital,' Nandan says. 'He should be up and about in a few days.'

'You left him all by himself?' Orko retorts, his tone sharper than he intends it to be.

'Well, Tenia is taking care of him,' says his father. 'Besides, your exams are just around the corner, and I have missed a week of classes.'

Orko is unnerved by his father's presence. 'Mashi!' he calls out to his aunt. 'Baba is here.' It's Sunday, and Nandan has brought with him the bags they use on their weekly trip to Gariahat market. When he called last night, he did say that he would be here this morning, and that they would go to the market together, but somehow Orko didn't quite register that this meant he was going back home today.

Sudeshna emerges from her bedroom. She smells of Neem soap, and her hair is wet. 'I'm glad your uncle is better now,' she says to Nandan. 'Orko has been a very good boy. We've done quite a bit of studying together.'

'That's good to hear,' says his father, eyeing the periodicals stacked on the shelf by the sofa.

It irks Orko when his father or his aunt speaks of him as if he's an infant. Of course, it's true that Orko has been fine. In fact, he hasn't felt so calm and collected in months. Just a week ago it had seemed to him that he was going to fail his board examinations. Now he thinks he's going to get by without too much of a struggle.

'I could do with some tea,' Nandan says, picking up yesterday's newspaper from the coffee table.

'Well, I don't have your fancy Darjeeling,' Sudeshna replies. 'I can fix you a cup of my daily poison.' It is as if the words are a part of a different conversation, one that Orko doesn't know the beginning of.

'That'll do just fine,' says Nandan, and he folds the newspaper to the editorial section and settles into a chair.

Orko can't think of anything to say to his father. He's feeling much better now, but he doesn't say this to Nandan, because Nandan doesn't know how he was feeling before he came here. He paces between the kitchen and the living room, unable to sit still.

'Have you packed all your books?' Sudeshna asks.

Orko hasn't packed his books, or his clothes. 'Can't I stay here?' he asks his aunt in a voice that's almost a whisper. Sudeshna is distracted by the whistle of the kettle. She says nothing. 'Just for a few more days?' Orko is desperate now. He means to whisper, but the words come out too loud.

Sudeshna glances at him as she pours the boiling water into a teapot. She looks ill at ease. 'Go home with your father,' she says. 'You can come and spend the weekend.'

'But I don't have to go to school until the exams,' Orko says. 'Study leave.'

'I'll come and help you with your studies,' says Sudeshna.

'But if I stayed here, you wouldn't have to come all the way every day,' he persists.

Sudeshna gives him a look that tells him it's futile to argue more. On a tray by the stove is a plate with biscuits and a cup on a saucer. Sudeshna places the teapot on the tray and carries it out of the kitchen. Orko follows her into the living room.

'Bring the teapoy closer to your father,' Sudeshna says to Orko. Nandan looks up from his newspaper. 'I'm arranging a Satyanarayan pujo for him,' she says to Nandan, as she places the tray on the teapoy.

Orko is surprised – he has been here all week, and this is the first he's hearing of the pujo. Nandan folds the newspaper carefully before putting it away. It's clear that he is displeased.

'I know you're a nonbeliever,' Sudeshna says. 'I don't care. You're to bring him to my house next Sunday, at nine.'

'There really isn't any need for all of that,' says Nandan. 'He's fine. Sit down and have some tea with me.'

'I've never imposed my beliefs on anybody,' says Sudeshna. 'This is an earnest request – indulge me, just this once.'

Nandan smiles at Sudeshna, and Orko knows that smile. When he was younger and he said something amusing, his father would smile at him like that.

'What are you smiling at me for?' Sudeshna demands. 'You think everything is a joke?'

'Go pack your bag,' she says to Orko. 'And don't come back here until you're called for.'

Orko gathers his books from the dining table and hurries away in search of the rest of his belongings. He stuffs everything he can find into his bag. It isn't as heavy as it had seemed when he left home with it. He wonders if he's forgetting something. He goes back towards the living room, to ask his aunt if any of his clothes are in the washing, but he stops short. They're still talking – about him, by the sound of it. The green curtain is thick enough that he's sure they can't see him.

'I don't see what's wrong with the football camp,' his father says. 'It seems to have done Orko a lot of good. He's more confident, more focused. He goes running every afternoon. I hear he shows a lot of promise.'

'That's a load of rubbish,' Sudeshna says. 'I taught adolescent boys for ten years. I know what they'll do to someone like Orko. You didn't think it necessary to ask me before sending him? Does my opinion count for nothing?'

'I think you worry too much. He's a big boy now,' Nandan says. 'Learning to play a team sport is very important. Besides, I'm sure he has made new friends at the camp.'

Orko can't bear to listen anymore. He walks away quietly, to his grandfather's room at the other end of the house. His head hurts. Did Bishu tell his father all those things about him? Did they meet, to exchange notes about his progress? Orko can think of no other way his father would know that he showed promise. None of the boys at the camp would have had anything good to say about him. Was his father a party to everything that had happened to him? Did his father ask Bishu to straighten him out, to teach him how to be a man? The very thought is so revolting that it makes his stomach turn.

As they walk away from Sudeshna's house, Nandan seems lost in thought. Orko feels ungrateful for wanting to remain with his aunt. He wishes he hadn't told her anything about the football camp. They walk past the cinema, and when they're at the traffic lights at the end of the avenue Nandan says: 'I thought you liked football. I don't know if you're aware of it, but since you joined the camp, your demeanour has changed. For the better, I should think.'

Orko is lost for words. He feels as if his father doesn't know him at all, and this, too, is entirely his fault. He thinks of all the times when Nandan asked him how he was, and 'Fine' was all he said. He wonders what his father would think if Orko told him the whole story. It is entirely a thought experiment, of course; he can never recount the whole story, to anybody.

As they walk towards Gariahat, Orko picks at the memories of the conversations he had with his aunt. It is an idle exercise; he isn't looking for anything in particular. Why was it that his father never spoke to him about his mother? Was it because he thought Orko was too young, or was it because it was too painful for him to talk about his late wife? Does his father miss his mother like he does? He pictures his father at the crematorium, chatting casually with his kinsmen about cricket and the Golden Temple, while his mother's body lies on a bier a few feet away. Moments later, he hates himself for conjuring up that image. He tries to obliterate it – every memory of it – from his consciousness. The truth is that his father is a kind man. He's a gentle man. He's a learned man. He's a respected professor at the university, and people come to him for advice about important things. He still finds the time to care for Orko, and to cook for him, and to ask after his wellbeing. It's just as well that Orko doesn't waste his father's time with complaints about his own petty predicaments.

They're in the fish market, and Nandan is paying for a kilo of pomfret. A year ago, Orko loved pomfret, just like his father. Now he loathes it. As a matter of fact, he never wants to eat fish again.

It's Sunday again, and Orko and his father are at his aunt's house. Nandan rings the bell; Orko stands behind him, hands clasped together.

'Thank you for coming,' says Sudeshna, holding the door open. 'The priest has been here for a while now.'

Orko steals a glance at the clock on the far wall. They're a few minutes late.

'I have some errands to run,' Nandan says. 'Orko can come home by himself after the circus.'

Orko cringes at his father's words, and Nandan leaves without saying goodbye. Orko follows his aunt to the balcony over the portico, where he spent so many afternoons with his grandfather. The balcony is unrecognisable now. In his memories, the windows are unadorned; there's the television set, with the little magic box by its side; Amiya's easy chair, the colour of ebony, about eight feet from the TV screen; Orko's little rattan chair, now two feet to the right of Amiya, now brushing up against his side; Amiya's hand in his – bony, trembling, encased in the softest skin.

Now the windows have white curtains, with lace trim. The spot where the television set used to be has been given over to the pujo. There's a foot-high table, set out with the usual appeasements – tiny plates laden with fruits; matching glasses filled with water; little mounds of raw rice, moist, each crowned by a slice of banana; a copper pot, its mouth gagged with a red towel, on which is a green coconut with a long, gnarly stalk like the horn of a unicorn. The priest sits on a rough handloom prayer mat. There are three more stacked in a corner. Sudeshna takes one, and hands another to Orko. She spreads her prayer mat to the left of the priest, but not directly alongside, as if in deference to his higher station. She motions to Orko to do the same. Orko sits to the right of the priest, in line with his aunt.

When he was little, Orko and his mother performed a Lokkhi pujo every year. It was always just the two of them. They awoke before daybreak on the morning of the pujo.

They drank the last glass of water they were allowed before the period of fasting began. They painted little footsteps, with paste made from chalk and rice dust. The footsteps led from their front door to every room in their flat. These were Ma Lokkhi's footsteps, his mother told him. They served as a guide for Ma Lokkhi, so she would know to visit every room, to bless its occupants. When the hour of the pujo drew near, his mother entrusted Orko with painting the remaining footsteps, while she worked on a large floral motif on the floor of the room where the pujo was to be performed. Ma Lokkhi's idol took centre stage, on a foot-high wooden platform. Around the seat of Ma Lokkhi there were offerings, much like the offerings at today's pujo. No priest invaded their private ceremony. His mother sat by Ma Lokkhi's seat, on a prayer mat much like the one on which Orko is sitting now. She closed her eyes and went through the entire set of incantations, swaying from side to side, as if in a trance.

Today, the priest pronounces the incantations in a monotonous drone. He clutches a bell in his left hand and rings it from time to time. He tosses a few flowers at the unicorn. He doles out handfuls of petals to Orko and his aunt, asking them to do the same. He pronounces a Sanskritised version of Orko's name thrice, in a verse that lasts about a minute. His aunt blows on a conch shell. The priest half-turns towards him and anoints him with sandalwood paste. Then he does the same to his aunt. He asks them to cover their feet. His aunt draws hers under the folds of her saree. Orko kneels, so his feet are hidden away. The priest sprinkles holy water on them. For peace, he says.

When they're done, his aunt squishes the fruit and the rice together into a paste, which she then serves to Orko in a bowl made of bone china. She serves herself a bowl too, and genuflects before raising a spoonful to her mouth. Orko knows from experience that he must do the same. He turns his face away so his aunt can't see him grimace. He gulps down the contents of the bowl with feigned gusto. He feels sick to the stomach. The paste reminds him of Bishu.

Seven

In December, the mornings are grey, the afternoons short and yellow, like the final moments of an ant drowning in a jar of honey. Sweaters, scarves and shawls emerge from the top shelves of wardrobes and from steel trunks stowed under beds. There's a faint smell of mothballs in minibuses and in doctors' chambers. Men and women scurry about the wispy morning streets, wrapped in their woollens of blue and yellow and brown. On Sundays they go to the Botanic Gardens and to the zoo, with sandwiches wrapped in old newspaper and thermos bottles of instant coffee, not quite piping hot. They recline on reed mats spread on the green, while their children play hide-and-seek or immerse themselves in adventures that can only take place in the pages of a book. Evening falls without warning. Feeble street lamps shine valiantly, illuminating huddled figures with plumes of cigarette smoke floating over their heads like speech bubbles in a comic book.

The grey mornings and the quick afternoons bleed into the new year, and the men and women spend their time and money at the fairgrounds by the maidan. They're in trams and buses with armloads of books, a heady new book smell about them. Late in the evening, they wrap themselves in their shawls and drink tea, piping hot, from earthen cups before spending the night seated on uncomfortable chairs in concert halls fashioned out of tarpaulins and bamboo scaffolding.

Orko can't remember a winter as idyllic as this one. His board exams are behind him. He is home, alone, swaddled in a soft shawl that had once belonged to his mother. The shawl is a fuzzy mauve, and it too smells of mothballs. The hours go by languidly, with Simon & Garfunkel playing on the stereo. Orko doesn't know how long he's been reading, only that it has been too long – the text on the page grows fuzzy, then fades into an unintelligible blur. He sets the book down by his pillow and contemplates his future, stringing together vignettes of an imagined adulthood. It's a frustrating exercise, because he can never place his future self in these vignettes.

Priya is born in a lazy, ill-considered moment, to take Orko's place in these imaginings. She lives here, in this room. Her given name is Orkopriya, but her mother called her Orko. She had chosen that name before Priya was born, in anticipation of a son. To her friends, though, she's Priya, because Orko is a boy's name.

In the beginning, Priya is just an apparition; a wraith who appears only in the dead of night, or early in the afternoon, when the world is bathed in honey. Orko isn't alarmed, because he knows her from the sketches in his mother's notebook. She reminds him of a song about moonbeams and fairytales. He watches her wistfully, enviously, with the knowledge that he is Orko and she is Priya, and that one could never be the other. She is graceful, like a ballerina, and he is like Pinocchio, his arms and legs held together with twine. She is self-assured – cocky, even – and he is the embodiment of infinite hesitation.

Priya has a wing, shaped like a butterfly's, and striped like a zebra. She can't fly on the one wing, of course, but she likes the way it looks. She pictures herself, naked, the wing resting against her shoulder blade. She wishes she had another wing so that she could fly away. She stands at the window, her wing in mourning for its lost twin. Orko wishes she would go away, and she does.

When she returns, she is no longer a wraith, and no longer benign. She begins to carve out portions of Orko's life and claim them for herself. Soon there's a poster of Boy George brushing up against Tracy Chapman, and by the stereo there's a jewelled box made of silver. Inside the box are four pairs of earrings. The little golden hoops are the only pair she's allowed to wear to school, but the ones she loves most are the silver owls that nestle against her earlobes. She only wears those in the evenings, because owls don't like grey mornings or yellow afternoons.

Priya taunts Orko with visions of futures that could never be his. She's a singer, and a songwriter. She plays the flute, the dulcimer, the guitar and the piano. She speaks French and Japanese, fluently. She's a mystery writer. She's the first human on Mars. She's a champion swimmer. She has two children, and she takes them swimming every afternoon.

Orko envies Priya, but it isn't because she's so accomplished, or because she has two children. He envies her for the secrets she shares during sleepovers at Urmi's, under a duvet so roomy that there's four of them in there, with room to spare. He resents her because she plays games with his memories, painting pictures of a past that might have been his if he were a girl. It's Priya who sat with Urmi on her terrace, reading, eating puffed rice and fighting over the boy in the book. Priya had her ears pierced first, and Urmi envied her for the beautiful earrings she wore to school. When she went swimming with her mother, she was never sent away to the men's changing rooms. When the boys on the football field taunted her with that jaded trope about cows and flowers, she had the last laugh; she ran circles around them during the game that followed. When Bishu asked her to take her clothes off, Priya chopped off his penis with a machete.

When the doorbell rings, Priya leaves, taking with her the poster of Boy George and the little jewelled box from beside the stereo, and Orko is left floundering, gasping, clutching at thin air in an effort to piece together a future in which he can participate as himself. He knows that he's never going be able to play the dulcimer or the flute, and he's not going to be an astronaut. He's never going to marry, or have children, or wear silver owls on his earlobes. Nevertheless, he decides that he isn't going to remain friendless and alone just because he isn't a girl; he isn't going to try to walk like a man, or sit or carry his books like one, because the idea that somehow one could learn to do that seems preposterous. He is tired of being afraid. He is going to go back to the football field, and he is going to run. He's going to become strong and confident, like his mother. In the meantime, if Bishu tries to speak to him, he is going to keep on running until he reaches home; Urmi's mother told her to run as fast as she could if strange men tried to talk to her.

It's a Monday morning, more golden than grey. Orko answers the door, and he's surprised to see Urmi. They haven't spoken in weeks. On the night after their last board exam, Urmi had a sleepover at her place. Nilanjana and Paromita were invited; he wasn't. Orko swallowed his pride and asked Urmi if he could come too, but Urmi said that it was girls only; she couldn't do anything about it because her mother said so. Orko didn't quite believe her, because he had spent the night at Urmi's in the past and her mother never seemed to mind. He considered asking Ketaki-mashi if she really didn't want him to spend the night, but he was afraid that he would discover it was Urmi who didn't want him.

Orko doesn't want to be the first to speak. He waits for Urmi to tell him why she's here, but she doesn't say anything either. Impatience gets the better of him, and he throws her a questioning glance.

'The results are out,' Urmi says. 'I'm going to school. Ma says I should ask if you wanted to come along.'

'Why don't you go with your friends?' Orko retorts. 'I'm sure they'll be happy to go with you.'

'Don't be an ass,' Urmi says. 'Do you want to come with me or not?'

Orko doesn't want to go to school. He's sure he has failed the chemistry test. He tries to construct the sentences that he's going to use to break the news to his father.

'Well?' Urmi asks impatiently.

Orko has half a mind to say something spiteful. He wants to tell her that it was terribly mean of her not to invite him that night, but he can't think of a way to say it without giving her the upper hand. 'Please be seated,' he says, in a tone he uses when addressing a visitor asking to see his father. 'I'll get dressed.'

As they walk to the bus stop, the bristling resentment begins to fade. He can see why Urmi didn't want him at the sleepover. Their friendship is hopelessly broken, and he's the one who broke it. The die was cast when he decided to go to the football camp just to spite her. When Bishu told him that he mustn't be friends with girls, it was Orko who began to distance himself from her. He stopped going for walks with her, and when she smiled at him he didn't smile back. In spite of it all, Urmi came looking for him this morning. She isn't going to be his classmate anymore, and they would probably drift further apart. In two years she would go away to college, like her brother. He would see her twice a year, when she came home for her vacations. He tries to frame an adequate apology as they ride the bus to Golpark, but every iteration seems hollow and facile.

Most of their classmates are in the compound when they arrive. There is animated conversation but Orko hears none of it. One of their teachers tells them that their marks have been posted outside the staffroom. Urmi forges ahead, threading her way through the huddles in the compound. Orko wants to be anywhere but here.

Outside the staffroom, about a dozen of their classmates jostle for a better view of the sheets plastered on the notice-board. Ten years of school, carved into capsules of time, precisely fifty minutes long; ink stains on his fingertips; notebooks covered in blue scribbles; annotations in red, from his teachers. None of it matters now. All that matters is on the noticeboard. There are nine lists – one for each subject. Each list has forty-nine names, in alphabetical order. Urmi is in the thick of things, notebook in hand. Orko is close enough to read the headers on the lists. English. Bengali. Mathematics. He looks away, at another board that says something about fees and deadlines.

'Here,' says Urmi, handing him a piece of paper as she emerges from the crowd. 'I wrote down your marks too.'

Orko folds the sheet and slips it into his pocket without looking at it.

Urmi gives him a surprised look. 'What's the matter with you?' she exclaims.

'Have I passed chemistry?' Orko asks.

'Why don't you see for yourself?' Urmi says. She doesn't sound exasperated anymore, and Orko finds this alarming. He feverishly digs the scrap of paper out of his trouser pocket. It's crumpled. Urmi reaches for Orko's hand just as he finishes straightening out the creases. 'I think you have the top score in English and in history,' she says.

Orko can barely hear her voice over the ringing in his ears. He only has forty-one out of a hundred marks in chemistry. He needed at least fifty in each of the science subjects to be in the science section. He has barely made the grade in mathematics and in physics, but that doesn't matter either. He's going to be in the humanities section.

In an instant, he remembers everything that anybody has ever said to him about studying humanities.

'It's going to get you nowhere,' said his chemistry teacher. 'You won't get a job. You'll spend the rest of your life teaching a bunch of losers how to make sentences and write essays.'

'They're all dolts,' Bodhi said dismissively of the girls in the humanities section. 'They can afford to study humanities because they're going to grow up and get married.'

Orko's head spins. He wishes he could sit down, but there aren't any chairs in the corridors. He realises that he hasn't asked Urmi about her results. 'Show me yours,' he says.

She brings out a neatly folded sheet of paper from her sling bag. She hands it to him reluctantly. Just a glance tells him that she probably has the highest aggregate in their class. There have been many occasions when Orko has been envious of Urmi, but now he feels happy for her. It's almost as if they're different kinds of creature, their destinies disjointed. He hugs her, without thinking. She's taken aback, but her arms tighten around him for a fraction of a second. He's surprised at himself. This is the first time he has hugged Urmi at school. At school, boys don't hug girls. It just doesn't happen.

'I'm so happy for you,' he says.

'These scores don't mean a thing,' Urmi says, after an awkward silence. 'I know that you have something special; something that I don't have. I've known this forever.'

Urmi's words ring in Orko's ears. It's true that they have known each other forever. He can't remember a time when he didn't know Urmi. He wishes she wouldn't bring up his scores, or their childhood. This is her moment, and she ought to be happy. She isn't, and that's only because his scores are so dismal. He wishes he hadn't come to school with her.

'It isn't as bad as all that,' he says. 'At least I won't make a fool of myself, trying to be an engineer.' He contrives a laugh that sounds terrible, and Urmi doesn't laugh with him. They walk, without really intending to, to the guava tree behind the main block. They sit on the parapet under the tree. They don't talk about the times when they were in that tree, just the two of them. They don't talk about the fact that Urmi is moving to a different school. They sit there quietly until they see Kaushik and Paromita come around the corner.

They exchange perfunctory greetings. Kaushik volunteers his scores. The rest of them congratulate him on doing so well, and Kaushik beams at them. Orko knows that Urmi's aggregate is higher, but he doesn't want to rain on Kaushik's parade.

Urmi and Orko make their way across the yard to the back gate. Kaushik and Paromita take their place under the guava tree. As they pass beneath the archway and out through the gate, Orko feels as if everything that is precious and familiar is slipping away from him.

'There's nothing to be dejected about,' Nandan says when Orko shows him the sheet of paper torn out of Urmi's notebook. 'It's not the end of the world. I see that you've done very well in English. I've been telling you all along that you should study literature.'

Orko had been steeling himself for the moment when he would have to tell his father how poorly he had done, and now that moment has come and gone. He remembers the time when Bodhi's results were declared. 'He could have done much better,' Bodhi's father lamented for weeks afterward. Every lost mark was analysed, every failing dissected, even though Bodhi, like Urmi, had the highest aggregate in his class. Orko's father, on the other hand, is laconically picking out bones from a portion of fish. Orko wishes that, for once, his father would say something. Anything would do. Anything at all.

'Everything happens for the best,' Nandan says as they're finishing dinner. 'Now you know what your strengths are.'

After dinner, for the first time in weeks, Orko clears the table without being asked. Just as he finishes wiping down the surface of the table, he notices a tiny speck of dal where his plate had been. He is so overcome by exhaustion that he can't bring himself to wipe it away. He leaves the dishcloth on the table and retreats to his room. He doesn't change into his pyjamas, and he doesn't brush his teeth. Although it is January, he's sweating under his collar. He switches on the fan before falling into bed.

He lies in the dark, staring at the faint disc of the ceiling fan as it whirrs overhead. He wishes there was music, but he hasn't the will to choose. He feels like throwing away all his cassettes, all his books, all his clothes, everything in his room. All through the school year, his teachers had gone on about how important these examinations were. Now the results are out; he has done poorly, and his father doesn't care enough to be angry with him. He wonders if it is because his father didn't expect any better from him.

He remembers the first time he felt this way. It was a holiday, and Orko was in the parking lot of their enclave, playing cricket. A stack of bricks served as the wicket, and another solitary brick, a few metres away, marked the bowler's crease. They were using a neon-green tennis ball that day, and Orko was last at the crease. He remembers the ball – fuzzy, bouncing unpredictably, darting at him. He faced just one delivery that day. Shubho lobbed it at him as he stood in front of the makeshift wicket, bat in hand. Just as the ball bounced, Orko saw his father out of the corner of his eye, watching them from a distance. He remembers the handle of the bat, with its textured rubber grip. He remembers the heft of it in his hands, just as it slid from his grasp and crashed into the stack of bricks. There was laughter all around. Shubho came up to him and said that the same thing had happened to him too, and that Orko mustn't cry.

He remembers searching for his father and realising he was gone. He remembers feeling relieved, and thinking for days that his father hadn't seen him make a fool of himself.

He can't remember if it was the very next Sunday when he overheard his father and his uncle, in the living room of their father's house. They were talking about him. 'The boy has absolutely no hand-eye coordination,' his father said, and the twelve-year-old Orko ran away, up flights of stairs that seemed to go on forever, to the terrace of his grandfather's house.

It's morning, and for a few moments Orko isn't sure what day of the week it is. He hopes it isn't Saturday. On Saturdays, Orko goes to Gariahat market with his father, to shop for provisions. Today Orko wants to stay in bed.

It turns out that it is, in fact, Saturday, but today they aren't going to Gariahat.

'Wear a good shirt,' Nandan says to Orko at breakfast. 'We're going to meet an old acquaintance of mine.'

At the back of the bottom shelf of Orko's wardrobe is a blue shirt. It is full-sleeved, and there's a pocket sewn onto the left breast. The shirt looks clean, but it is creased, like a crumpled old newspaper. Someone had gifted this shirt to his father a few years ago, but it was too small for Nandan. Orko irons it, and when he slides his arms into the sleeves, they're still warm. He doesn't like wearing shirts like these. They make him feel as if he's walking about in a cardboard box, or in someone else's skin. He avoids looking in the mirror as he tucks the shirt into his trousers.

'You're looking civilised for a change,' says Nandan when Orko walks out of his room. 'Let's go.'

Orko has no idea where they're going. They walk to the rickshaw stand near the playground. When Nandan negotiates the fare with the driver, Orko doesn't recognise the destination. They ride in silence for a distance, until Orko asks his father who they are meeting, not because he's curious but because the silence is making him uncomfortable.

This is when his father tells him that he's going to enrol Orko for typing lessons.

'I'm worried about you,' Nandan says. 'I won't be able to support you forever. I'm going to grow old, and then I'm going to retire. Eventually, I'm going to die, and they'll stop my pension. You need to have a vocation in order to be able to fend for yourself.'

Orko can't think of anything to say. Everyone he knew went to college after they finished school. His father must think that no college would have him. He can't bring himself to say that he is going to do well from now on, and that the chemistry test is an aberration.

When Orko was younger, his father sometimes took Orko to his office. Mrs Barman, the typist, would save her dessert for him and bring it to him on a saucer, with a spoon that looked like it was a hundred years old. As he sat there, in one of the two chairs across the desk from his father, she would take sheafs of foolscap paper with his father's handwriting from the blue tray on the desk. Orko would do his homework to the clacking of the typewriter in the distance. Sometimes he would race the typewriter, rushing to complete a line of longhand in the interval between two rings of the carriage return. When it was time for them to leave, Mrs Barman would return with a neat stack of typed sheets. She would smile at Orko, waving a silent goodbye as she left the room. His father would continue working, without so much as a glance to acknowledge her presence.

'I want to be a professional typist,' Orko imagines himself saying the next time one of his teachers asks their class if they have given any thought to what they want to do when they grow up. He wonders if the teacher would join his classmates in laughing at him.

They come to a halt outside a two-storey house on a narrow, unfamiliar lane. There are clothes hung out to dry on the first-floor balcony. A weathered sign, affixed above the cornice, reads 'Regent Commercial Institute'. The front door is open; inside, there's an overpowering smell of fish frying. The room looks like it was once a drawing room. There are bookshelves built into the walls, and behind their sliding glass doors are compendia of the works of Tagore, Sarat Chandra, Shakespeare. There are books by Robert Ludlum and by Alistair MacLean. There are no sofas or armchairs, and there's no coffee table. The floor space is almost entirely given over to three writing desks crammed together, each sporting an ancient Remington typewriter, like the one Mrs Barman had before she got her computer. The accompanying chairs look like they belong around a dining table. Against the far wall are four green chairs made of plastic. On the table closest to the front door is a stack of newspapers. The paperweight is actually a mechanical bell, with a plunger that effects a half-hearted tinkle when pushed. Orko's father has one of those on his table. He uses it to summon Mrs Barman when he wants something typed, or when he can't find some papers he had left on his desk.

Nandan rings the bell twice, just like he does in his own office. 'Sit,' he says to Orko, motioning towards the chairs lined up against the wall. He picks up a newspaper and sits in the chair beside Orko. Orko tries to picture the person they're waiting for. He tries to deduce if his father has been here before, but he can't conclude one way or another. He wishes his father would put down the newspaper and tell him that this is a charade, designed to scare him into studying harder.

They wait there in the strange room for ten minutes before a man enters through the door at the back, clearing his throat as he glances in their direction. By the sound of it, it doesn't seem like his throat actually needs clearing. When his father greets the man, Orko gathers that his surname is Mukherjee, and his father knows him only in passing.

They follow Mukherjee-babu through a door that leads into another room lined with more tables that have typewriters on them, then through another door into a tiny windowless room lit by a bare fluorescent tube. The light is harsh and excessive, and Orko squints until his eyes stop hurting. In this room is an oversized writing table. Mukherjee-babu motions at the two chairs nearest them. As they take their seats, he squeezes through the narrow gap between the table and the wall and takes his place in the stuffed chair opposite them. He smiles at Orko, then clears his throat again.

'Orko,' he says, to no one in particular. 'I like the name.' He turns to Orko, although he should have actually addressed Orko's father, because Orko had no part in choosing that name. He asks Nandan if he would like some tea, and Nandan nods. Mukherjee-babu calls for three cups of tea, without asking Orko if he would like some.

Orko gathers from the conversation that they're living in difficult times. Offices and factories are shutting down because the communist government is encouraging workers to strike, and jobs are hard to come by, especially for students who haven't done well in school. Mukherjee-babu commends Orko's father for his foresight, emphasising that Orko is the youngest student he has ever had; people usually came to him after they have finished college and failed to find a job, or failed the civil services examinations. From all of this, Orko gathers that his father had called ahead and given Mukherjee-babu some background about why he wanted Orko to take typing lessons. He is sure that he wouldn't be sitting here in this dank, windowless room if he had done well in the board examinations, like Bodhi, or like Urmi. He is here because his father has already decided that the best he can do is spend a lifetime typing out other people's words onto reams of letter paper.

On his first day back at the football field, Orko is apprehensive. It is too early for Bishu to be here, but some of the boys from the camp are on the field, aimlessly kicking a ball about. Orko is wearing a new pair of sneakers. He didn't ask his father to buy them for him; he emptied out the biscuit tin in which he keeps the savings from his pocket money. He thinks about all the cassettes he could have bought instead of the ill-fitting sneakers.

Soon after he begins to run, one of the boys notices him and lets out a hoot. A voice that's vaguely familiar calls out his name. Another calls him a cow, then a bitch. He keeps on running; they're less likely to accost him if he ignores them, he reasons. By the fifth lap, his mind latches onto the steady pounding of his feet on the earthen track. He becomes acutely aware of the building stress in his muscles, of the sweat that runs into the small of his back. The back of his neck is hot, and he feels the occasional chill down his spine. The catcalls fade away. By the tenth lap, he is tired enough that he has to watch his loosely clenched fists and imagine they are little pistons propelling him forward. His mind is bare now; it is almost as if he's in a trance, waking only to advance the counter as he goes past the flagpole at the corner of the field, then falling back into the trance again.

He remains in the trance as he walks back home and up the stairs to the flat. He switches on the fan in the living room and lies on his back on the cold mosaic floor. He feels invincible as he lies there, his arms spread out like the wings of a kite, tracing lazy spirals against an azure sky.

The call to prayer from a faraway mosque reminds him that it will soon be time for typing school. He wishes he didn't have to go, but he hasn't worked up the courage to tell his father that he doesn't want the lessons. He picks himself off the floor and makes his way to the bathroom.

He takes his clothes off. As he steps out of his briefs, he forgets to look away, and sees the penis between his legs. He has the distinct sensation that his body is not really his own. When this happens, he usually pinches his forearm to reassure himself that he is alive, and real. Today, his fingertips have no sensation, and he feels as if somebody else's fingers just brushed against his forearm.

On his haunches, he pours a mug of cold water on his head. It rolls past the back of his neck, down his spine and over the small of his back, before glancing off his tailbone. There's no mistaking that it is, indeed, his neck, his spine, the small of his back and his tailbone. The penis, on the other hand, doesn't belong. It's ugly, and it's inconvenient.

When the first drops of water trickle down to his groin, he feels nothing at all.

At the typing school, Mukherjee-babu greets him and sets him an assignment. *The quick brown fox jumps over the lazy dog.* The soft bell of the carriage return. Then the fox jumps again. The cycle repeats, like a Buddhist monk fingering his prayer beads. The spell is broken when he inadvertently presses down on two keys at the same time. The type bars become entangled; they remind him of a frightened crab, tripping over its own legs as it scurries across the sand.

Eight

On the first day of the new school year, Orko discovers that he is the only boy in his class. As they queue up for assembly, Kaushik shouts out to him: 'Hey, Orko, why are you standing there with the girls?' Orko pretends not to hear any of it, but Kaushik won't give up. He suggests that Orko change his name to Orkie. The name sounds so ridiculous that Orko begins to laugh. This seems to throw Kaushik off, and he turns his attention to Sugato's oily hair. The bell rings and the voices die down. The principal addresses them and, after the usual exhortations and a few announcements, they all sing the school anthem.

Afterwards, as Orko makes his way to his new classroom, two of his former classmates overtake him on the stairs. They lower their voices as they approach, and one of them scoffs as they pass him. Orko slows down momentarily, to put some distance between himself and the two boys. He tells himself that they can't possibly be talking about him, but he isn't convinced.

The classroom seems larger than usual, but that's only because it has been provisioned for fewer students than Orko is used to. There are six desks, arranged in two rows. Each desk seats two, so there are twelve seats in all. At the threshold of his new classroom, Orko misses Urmi desperately. In the ten years that he has been in school, Urmi has always been in his class. They've shared a desk for nine of those years. With her gone, he feels unhinged.

Nilanjana is in the seat closest to the door. Orko would probably choose to sit with her, but she is sharing her desk with Paromita. They smile at Orko as he walks in. Orko smiles back. Strangely enough, the front row is fully occupied. Shreya and Nandini are at the desk in the centre. Farah and Ishani are in the far corner. Behind them, in the seat by the window, is a girl he has never seen before.

The new girl is paler than anyone Orko has met. She's wearing steel-rimmed glasses, like John Lennon's. Her hair is almost as short as his own, and she isn't wearing earrings. Orko doesn't want to sit by himself, but he can't bring himself to ask the new girl if he can sit beside her. What if she'd rather sit alone, and is too polite to turn him down? He sets his schoolbag down on the desk beside hers, and just as he's about to sit down she looks up at him.

'Hi,' she says. 'I'm Brishti.'

There's something unfamiliar about the way she says the words. He knew another Brishti, and he remembers that she pronounced her name differently. She holds out her hand, and Orko shakes it.

'My name is Orko,' he says tentatively. Her grip is firm, and he, in turn, clasps her hand tightly before letting go.

'This seat's free,' she says, pointing, with her eyes, to the chair beside her. Orko sits down, forgetting that his schoolbag is on the neighbouring desk.

Mrs Sanyal (they address her as Nandita-di) walks into their classroom. She announces that she's going to be their class teacher this year. Orko likes Nandita-di. Last year, Orko had used a fragment of a song in an essay; she told him that she too liked the song, but it was lazy of him to use other people's words to express himself.

Nandita-di starts by welcoming them to their new class. She ticks off their names in the attendance register. She asks Brishti to introduce herself, and Orko learns that Brishti grew up in Canada, that she lives with her father, who is a pilot, and that her favourite book is *The Catcher in the Rye*.

Orko is more than a little amused when Nandita-di announces that the first book they're going to read this year is *Lord of the Flies*.

As days go by, Orko begins to enjoy school again. The awkwardness of being the only boy in his class fades away, and he's relieved that he no longer has to study mathematics or chemistry. Kaushik tried to rile him up a few times during the first week. Orko ignored him, and now he doesn't bother Orko anymore.

Orko quite likes sitting next to Brishti. On most days they're the only ones in the classroom during the lunch break, and he knows now that her parents are divorced, that she lives close by, with her father, and that her mother, whom she misses terribly, lives in Montreal. Orko wishes that he, too, could talk about himself, but he doesn't know how. He has managed to tell her that he lives with his father, and that his mother died when he was eight. He hasn't told her about Urmi. He hasn't told her about his favourite books, because he's scared that he'll end up talking about how he dwells in their pages, because in those pages he's Emma, or Geraldine, or Anne. He's so afraid of giving himself away that he lies for no reason at all. Although he no longer plays football, he tells Brishti that he enjoys the game, and that he's very good at it. He finds a copy of *The Catcher in the Rye* in a dusty old bookshop on the boulevard. He doesn't really like the book, but he tells her that he read it four times over a weekend, and that it is now one of his favourite books.

Orko doesn't think of Bishu often, but when he does he feels angry, and stupid for having distanced himself from his friends on Bishu's advice. He occasionally visits Urmi, but she's usually busy and they don't really talk anymore. Nilanjana seems to have forgiven him, but Paromita still looks at him askance when he tries to talk to her.

Brishti is wearing earrings today, and Orko is surprised because she never wears earrings. He tries to persuade himself that it doesn't matter, and that earrings are frivolous, but he can't get over the fact that he's the only one in the class who isn't wearing any. It's almost as if they're the emblems of a secret club that will never accept him. As soon as the long bell signals the lunch break, Brishti takes out a book from her bag. It's a hardbound volume, covered in brown paper.

'What are you reading?' Orko asks.

'A book,' she replies as she opens the book about a quarter of the way from the end. She leafs through a few pages before beginning to read.

Orko walks over to Nilanjana's desk with his tiffin box.

'Hey, stranger!' she says. Orko smiles. 'Why don't you pull up a chair?'

'So you're back,' Paromita says, arching an eyebrow. They arrange their tiffin boxes on the desk, like an ersatz lunch buffet. There's a pear, cut into four, crackers, cheese sandwiches, and noodles. Soon, they're chatting away, like they used to, and Orko wishes Urmi was with them. They talk about the subjects they have to study, as if they're household chores assigned them. They talk about the students in the science section, and about their teachers. Their class teacher, who teaches them English literature; their history teacher, who always looks like she's just been woken from a siesta and isn't too happy about it; their young economics teacher, Debashish. His beard, just like George Michael's. His motorcycle. His beautifully tailored clothes.

'He's so cute,' says Paromita.

'Oh yes, he is, isn't he?' says Orko, blushing. Every time Debashish walks into their classroom, there's a flutter in Orko's heart.

'Maybe he'll ask you to marry him,' Paromita retorts.

The girls giggle, and this irritates Orko.

'Is that all you ever talk about, kissing and getting married and having babies?' The words come out of him in a rush.

Paromita is quick to come up with a rejoinder. 'Orko wants to kiss Debashish-da,' she says in a singsong voice and bursts out laughing. 'He wants to have a baby!' Nilanjana seems embarrassed, but Paromita continues to laugh.

Orko quickly looks around the classroom. He's relieved that there's just the three of them here, besides Brishti, who seems completely absorbed in her book. He walks back to his seat, leaving his empty tiffin box on the desk.

Brishti looks up from her book. 'You okay?' she asks. Orko nods, even as he senses his cheeks turning crimson.

Nilanjana brings Orko his tiffin box. 'She was just joking, you silly boy,' she says affectionately.

Orko doesn't respond. He focuses his attention on a whorl in the wooden surface of his desk. The bell signals the end of the interval, and the rest of the class trickles in. Orko is convinced that, before the end of the school day, Paromita is going to tell every one of them about their exchange. She's probably going to tell Kaushik too, and soon the whole school is going to think that he has a crush on Debashish.

Orko can't fathom his classmates' new-found obsession with romance and with relationships. All he had done was say that Debashish was cute. Anyone might have said that. It was a harmless, generic observation. Why did Paromita have to twist it around like that?

Among his classmates, Paromita is the only one who actually has a boyfriend. She and Kaushik usually leave school together. When they're a safe distance away, their hands come together and their pace becomes leisurely. As they walk down the footpath, Kaushik seems larger than life, and Paromita more diminutive. Kaushik's collar looks a little sharper than usual, his shoulders pulled back. His left hand finds its way to his trouser pocket as his right encircles Paromita's waist. Paromita seems slender, her upper arms pressed firmly against her sides, her fingers playing with the end of her long plait, as if it were the hand fan from the Japanese painting that hangs in Nandan's bedroom. Kaushik's glance falls on the side of Paromita's face, while Paromita's is cast downwards, at the ground that lies a few feet ahead of her. From time to time she steals a furtive glance at him, as if she can't bear to look at him for too long.

Orko has seen them at the tea stall near Golpark, sitting side by side on the makeshift bench. Kaushik sips his tea from a glass tumbler, Paromita from an earthen cup. He has always wondered what they talk about. They have nothing in common. When she's with her friends, Paromita is always talking about the latest movies from Bollywood, about how gorgeous Aamir Khan is, and about Madhuri Dixit's outfit in that lurid song in which she heaves about in the hay as the hairy Anil Kapoor gazes into her eyes, his fingers planted in the small of her back. Kaushik and his friends talk about football, about Jackie Chan, and about the new Sherlock Holmes show on television. Kaushik's friends refer to Paromita as Kaushik's wife, and Paromita doesn't protest. Orko wonders if they kiss. He's more or less certain they don't have sex, because Paromita's parents are very strict. If they knew that she spent time alone with Kaushik, even if it was just to walk hand in hand from their school to Golpark, they would probably ground her for the rest of her life.

Orko imagines Kaushik and Paromita as grown-ups, and he remembers the times when he spent the night at Urmi's. Her father went to the market in the morning, with two large nylon shopping bags. When he returned, the bags were bulging with vegetables and fish. Then he went for his bath, while Urmi's mother hurriedly prepared his breakfast and his tiffin. While she was in the kitchen, he sometimes called out to her from their bedroom. A misplaced shirt; a loose button; a pair of trousers that needed ironing. She rushed to his rescue, dropping whatever it was that she had been doing, returning in a mad frenzy after the crisis had been resolved. By the time Urmi's father walked out of the bedroom in a crisply ironed shirt and dark trousers, there was a placemat at the head of the table, a steel plate with a mound of rice in the shape of the dome of the planetarium, stainless-steel bowls with dal, two kinds of vegetables and fish curry, potato fritters near the edge of the plate, a stainless-steel tumbler full of water to the left of the plate, and a glass jug within easy reach from the seat at the head of the table, but not close enough that it got in the way. Urmi's father never touched the jug. When he wanted his glass refilled, he looked to his wife and she filled it for him.

Perhaps Kaushik and Paromita would grow up to be like Urmi's parents. They would get married and have two children – a boy and a girl. Kaushik would go to work every morning, and Paromita would stay home and look after their children.

When his mother was alive, Orko imagined that he was going to grow up to be exactly like her. He would have a husband – a bearded man, with curly hair. It would be nice if the man wore spectacles, but it wouldn't be terrible if he didn't. They would have two daughters, and Orko would take them swimming every day. Now, of course, he knows that he's not going to grow up to be a woman – he has a penis. If he didn't have one, maybe he would like to kiss Debashish, and then lie with him in bed, naked.

Sometimes, when Orko wakes in the morning, the penis is hard, and it pulses in time with his heart. He curls up, turning on his side, pressing his thighs around the penis until it doesn't ache anymore. When he looks at his groin (and he does this every time), the penis is gone. It's almost as if Ma Lokkhi had finally answered his prayer from the time when he still believed in her. Everything is possible now, and he can be anybody he wants to be – a dancer, or an astronaut, or a champion swimmer. He can play the flute and he can play the piano. In an exhilarating moment, Orko becomes Priya. She's not a boy anymore – she never was.

A bearded man appears by the window. He's naked, his skin taut against his slender frame, his clavicle and the contour of his ribcage plainly visible. There's a tuft of hair on his chest, and another, denser, just below his abdomen. His penis is strident, majestic even; Priya can't imagine that she ever thought it an ugly, useless appendage. When the man removes his spectacles and places them on the bookshelf, Priya's pulse begins to race. She studies each movement of his body as he takes the few strides that bring him to her bedside.

When he lies down beside her, she can barely breathe. He begins tentatively, kissing her lips, teasing her nipple with his fingertips, and she can tell, by the way he touches her, that the man is nothing like Bishu. He isn't as heavy as Bishu, and when he moves against her body, she moves with him. He doesn't grunt like a pig, even when his thrusts are at their most urgent and his eyes have glazed over. She doesn't recoil in disgust when his semen spills onto her thighs. Afterwards, they lie together; the man on his back, Priya on her side, an arm and a leg thrown over his torso. She doesn't know the man's name. They never speak, because Priya can't imagine what they would talk about. She doesn't even like the man very much. He has hairy arms and, like Bishu, he smells of stale underwear.

Orko was ten years old when their neighbour, Mr Sen, brought home a parrot in a rusty old cage from the fairground near Sealdah station. He called her Benazir. She was green, with a bright red beak. The first few times that Orko met Benazir, she sat sullenly in her cage.

Sometime after she arrived (maybe it was a week, or maybe it was two – Orko can't remember), Mr Sen bought her a new cage. This was a grand affair that looked like a teepee glued onto the top of a bucket. The bars were of a golden hue. Inside was a swing that hung from two lengths of silver chain. The cage had two doors: one for Benazir, and another, smaller, for her food.

Orko would ring his neighbours' doorbell every afternoon. 'Has she learned to speak yet?' he would ask.

'She's still young,' Mrs Sen would say. 'She'll learn.'

Mrs Sen told Orko how his mother worried when he was a baby. 'You didn't speak until you were almost two,' she said. 'All babies are different, I would tell your mother.' She looked at Orko and smiled. 'Look at you now!'

Orko would sit by the cage, watching Benazir intently. Mrs Sen would bring two plates on a tray – biscuits for Orko, and chillies, red and green, for Benazir. Orko would hold a chilli out for Benazir, but she would never bite it until he let it fall to the floor of the cage. She would approach it one step at a time, then cock her head, as if to make sure no one was looking, before partaking of it.

At the time, Orko had just finished reading a Tintin adventure, *The Broken Ear* – a birthday present from Kundan, his father's friend. One afternoon, Mrs Sen was away in the kitchen, and Orko didn't think she would hear him over the clatter of pots and pans. He walked up to the cage, and in a squeaky voice said, 'Great greedy guts,' just like the parrot from the Tintin book. Benazir didn't pay him any mind. She sulked. She opened and closed her beak noiselessly. Orko looked on with fascination at the bulge in her throat that moved up and down, like a live creature.

Orko went to see Benazir every day. Every day he would stand by her cage, feeding her chillies, red and green, and squawking 'Great greedy guts' at the mystified bird. Crows and sparrows would come sit at the window, like humans lined up to see an exotic creature at the zoo. Orko felt an urge to undo the clasp that kept Benazir. He wondered if she remembered how to fly.

'We've tried teaching her the names of the gods and goddesses,' Mrs Sen said one day, as Orko renewed his endeavour to teach Benazir that phrase which he thought must come naturally to a parrot. It was true that Benazir was green and the parrot in the comic book was red, blue and grey – but surely there must be something all parrots shared, irrespective of their colour?

'He's so gullible,' Mrs Sen said of her husband, when Benazir refused to speak in spite of all their efforts.

One day, as Orko sat on a stool by Benazir's cage, absent-mindedly passing red chillies to Benazir through the grille, she made a noise that was not her usual squawk. It sounded like an unremarkable twitter, different in tone and texture from the cuckoo's call, or the pigeon's, or the sparrow's, but bird-speak nevertheless. Then, she did it again, a little more spaced out this time.

'Great greedy guts,' she said, in a conspiratorial undertone.

'Great greedy guts,' Orko replied, barely containing his delight.

'Great greedy guts,' said Benazir again, rising to a fever pitch this time. 'Great greedy guts,' she said again and again, until Mrs Sen rushed in from the kitchen, staring at them in obvious glee. She clapped her hands. She brought Orko a cheese sandwich and said, 'Now teach her to say "Hare Krishna" and "Lokkhi Lokkhi".'

One afternoon a week or so later, Orko went to visit Benazir, only to find that the cage was empty. 'She's flown away,' Mrs Sen said to him. At the time Orko had been surprised, but now he feels positive that Benazir hadn't flown away. She had died in her golden cage, of heartbreak probably. He remembers how she would, in the first days that he knew her, look past the grille of her cage, as if she didn't quite understand that it was there. He wonders if it is possible for a creature to learn the language of another kind of creature. When he was a young child he would bark at dogs, mew at cats, moo at cows. There were no thoughts accompanying the sounds he made. He didn't feel like a cat when he mewed. The cows didn't pay him any mind as he mooed at them. The dogs sometimes barked back, but it sounded more like they had caught him out as an impostor than a response.

When Orko imagines himself as an adult, living and working in a world run by his schoolmates and by the boys at the football field, he wonders how long it will be before he is found out, and if it is worth the effort to continue pretending that he is like everyone else. In his most hopeful moments, he imagines that everyone is as weird as he is, keeping up this charade of sameness, terrified of revealing their true selves.

'Nobody wants war,' his grandfather had said to him once as they watched the Republic Day parade on television. 'But there will always be armies, because no one has the courage to be the first to throw away their weapons.'

Nine

It is afternoon, and the sky is a hazy shade of grey. The sounds of the street blend into a diffused hum. Everything seems blurry and faraway – the people on the footpath; the shanties with makeshift awnings fashioned out of tarpaulin, blue and yellow; the trams and the buses waiting impatiently at the traffic signal; the woman flagging down an auto-rickshaw.

Orko struggles to pay attention to the traffic as he crosses the busy street. His shoes are more scuffed than usual, from kicking at pebbles, paper cups and other detritus left behind on the streets by the people who walked them before him. The horn of a scooter buzzes behind him. He steps sideways onto the narrow footpath, startled. The scooter whizzes past, disappearing around a corner. Orko is disoriented – the street seems familiar, but not quite. He has never been here before.

The footpath curves into an unfamiliar lane. At the corner is a tubewell. Orko lets his fingers graze against its rusty handle as he passes it. There's a shop across the street, its shutters pulled down halfway to indicate that the minder is having a siesta. A man sleeps by his rickshaw on a makeshift bed fashioned out of sheets of old newspaper. The houses look alive, towering over him, watching his every move through their slatted eyes, casting barely discernible shadows on the pavement. A tabby cat crosses the lane and steps onto the footpath. It doesn't look like the strays Orko usually encounters when he's walking these lanes. It reminds him of an illustration in a book of nonsense rhymes that he read as a child, only the illustration was done in black and white, so he has no way of knowing what colour that cat had been.

The cat looks up at Orko, unafraid. It waits until Orko is just a few paces away, and Orko sees that its eyes are grey. It heads down the footpath, in no particular hurry. Orko decides to follow the cat; it doesn't seem to be out wandering – there's an unmistakable sense of purpose in its manner. The cat heads into an alley, where the air is hauntingly still. Orko realises that he is now completely lost.

The cat crosses the alley and comes to a halt in front of a closed door, flanked by a window on either side. There's a concrete bench to the left of the door. The cat leaps silently onto the bench, then up to the ledge of the window, before disappearing into the house through a missing windowpane.

Under normal circumstances, Orko wouldn't dream of looking in the window of someone's home, but these aren't normal circumstances. The windowpanes are dusty, some of them papered over. On the sill is a blue ceramic pot with a cactus in it. There's a table in the far corner, loose sheets of paper scattered on its surface. The walls look like they haven't been painted in a century. There doesn't seem to be a way out of the room; the cat seems to have vanished into thin air.

Outside, everything is disconcertingly unfamiliar. While he was following the cat, the street had seemed narrower, the light softer. Now the house on the other side of the street looks further away than it did a few moments ago. It casts a sharp shadow on the street, as if it was high summer and an early-afternoon sun was behind the house. The sky, though, is grey, like it has been all afternoon. Orko blinks, and the shadows are gone.

He thrusts his hands into his pockets and empties their contents. There's a handkerchief, a few coins, a ten-rupee note and a stick of gum. Orko counts the money, but it's nowhere near enough. He couldn't possibly leave home, forever, with just thirteen rupees on him. The contents of his schoolbag would probably fetch him a tidy sum at the second-hand shops along the boulevard, but the bag is still at his desk. His tiffin box, its contents untouched, is lying by the guava tree in the schoolyard. He thinks about the events that led him to leave school without his belongings, bringing him to the threshold of this mysterious house. He sits down on the bench, exhausted. He feels incapable of forming the intent to get back on his feet.

It all began to go wrong yesterday, when Debashish walked into their class. He *was* rather handsome, Orko thought, as Debashish proceeded to clean the blackboard, slowly, methodically, wiping down a quarter of the board with the chalk duster, pausing to tap the dust onto the shelf beneath, then turning his attention to the next quarter. Orko glanced at Paromita out of the corner of his eye, and when their glances met Orko thought she smirked at him.

From there it was all downhill. Every time Debashish looked in his direction during the class, Orko's muscles tensed, and he involuntarily looked towards the door. By the end of the class his ears were ringing and his head hurt.

After Debashish left their classroom, Orko tried to strike up a conversation with Brishti, but the words seemed contrived, and soon they were quiet again. He sat at his desk, staring at an open textbook, pretending to study. Brishti spent the lunch break reading *The Silmarillion*. Orko had read the book many times, but he didn't make any attempt to start a conversation about it.

Today, during the assembly, Orko felt as if everyone was staring at him, quietly mocking him, smirking at him behind his back. He forgot the words of the school anthem, and as the whole school joined in the cacophonous chorus, Orko looked straight ahead, his gaze burning a hole in the back of Farah's head. He glanced about furtively, and it seemed that many of his schoolmates were, in fact, watching him. He spoke to no one all morning, and he avoided making eye contact with anybody.

He seriously considered feigning illness and asking to be excused, but he didn't, because he felt sure they wouldn't let him go home by himself if he said he was ill. They would call his father at the university, and Nandan would have to come to the school to take him home. What was the matter with him, his father would ask. When did he start feeling unwell? Was it something he ate? Should they be seeing a doctor? Orko would have to spin yet another web of lies, and he didn't feel up to it.

During the break, he couldn't bear to sit in the classroom. He took his tiffin box out of his bag, and when he was halfway down the stairs he realised that he had forgotten his napkin. He instinctively began to turn back, but couldn't bring himself to go and fetch it. He continued down the stairs, past the staffroom, through the hall and out into the schoolyard. He spotted some of his former classmates bouncing a football. They had their backs to him. He quickly turned around and made his way to the back of the building, where the swings were.

Kaushik and Pratik were on the swings, but they weren't swinging. They had something in their hands, something they hid away the moment they saw him approach. From the acrid smell in the air he guessed that it was a cigarette they had just put out. He felt embarrassed for having walked in on their secret moment. As he turned to leave, Kaushik called out to him. Orko, without thinking, broke into a run.

'Hey!' Kaushik yelled. 'Come back here!'

'We aren't going to eat you up,' Pratik taunted.

Orko stopped in his tracks. He walked back towards the swings, slowly, with an air of calm confidence. He didn't want the boys to know how terrified he actually felt. He can't imagine that he will ever forget what happened next. He will remember the exact spot where it happened, the position of the shadow cast by the guava tree, the patch between his hairline and his collar where the sun warmed his skin.

'Why did you come here, homo boy?'

Kaushik's slur didn't really register at first. More than anything else, Orko felt indignant. He turned to leave but they called after him, asking him to come back. He ought to have run back to the safety of his classroom, pretending that he hadn't heard them.

'You like sucking dick, eh!' Kaushik spat when Orko wouldn't respond.

Orko was flabbergasted. For a moment he didn't understand why this was happening. Just as he thought of protesting, images of the room on the terrace flashed before his eyes. He was naked, with Bishu. They could see him in his nakedness, doing exactly the thing that they were accusing him of.

The rest of it unfurled in a blur of grey sky, a barrage of kicks and punches, flesh on grey flesh, black boots on grey trousers. He was face-down in the dirt. There were whoops. There was fading laughter.

Orko didn't return to his classroom after lunch. He sat in the guava tree, thinking about the time he had spent on its boughs with Urmi. He missed those times, and he missed her – the careless laughter, the bickering about the boy detective, the dolls' houses, the make-believe. It was all gone, forever. All that remained was self-loathing, shame and crushing loneliness.

Deep in the bowels of the mysterious house, a cuckoo announces that it is now four o'clock. Somehow, that doesn't seem right. Orko has no watch, so he can't be sure what time it really is. In all this time, he hasn't seen a soul. He feels as though he has stumbled through a secret passageway into a world of dark magic, where he is completely alone. For a moment, he considers ringing the doorbell. He could always say that he was lost, and ask for directions. He looks through the window but there's nobody in the room. The cat is fast asleep on the desk in the far corner. It looks smaller than it did on the street.

Orko is a little unnerved now. He walks away as fast as he can. Without thinking, he turns right at the end of the alley. He follows the lane for a few minutes, but it ends in a cul-de-sac. He retraces his steps, blundering mindlessly through the lanes until, incredibly, he finds himself at Golpark.

The bus pulls up just as he is about to reach the stop. He runs the last few metres. Getting on is a struggle. There are no seats available; there's barely room to stand. Riding with him in the rickety old minibus are clerks, bank managers, salesmen, all on their way home from their jobs at government offices, banks and shops. A mother is with her son, probably heading home from a tutorial. Orko can't imagine himself growing up to be like any of them.

Many years ago he had asked his grandmother, indignantly, why everyone had to go to school, then to college, only to get a job, get married and have children. She answered him with a quote from Shakespeare – it was all an act, she said, and his part had been written long before his parents had even met one another. All he had to do was follow the script. Orko still nurses a deep loathing for Shakespeare; when they read him at school, he tries to concentrate on the cadence of the words rather than their meaning.

Orko hates fish. He hates picking out the bones with his fingers, and he hates it even more when a tiny bone makes its way into his mouth. The smell nauseates him. When his father cooks fish the whole house stinks, and the stench bleeds into his clothes, his skin, his hair. It hangs about him as he peels away the skin from the slice on his plate. He breaks off a morsel with his fingers, mashing down the flesh, gingerly picking out the bones and laying them by the side of his plate before gathering up the shreds of flesh and bringing them to his mouth. His father takes his time. Charm, chew, masticate, swallow. Lick fingertips and repeat. Orko protests strenuously when he is offered a second helping. He imagines lying in bed after dinner, the smell leaching into the sheets and seeping into the mattress as he struggles to escape from its clutches.

There was a time, not so long ago, when Orko loved fish. He was driven to distraction when his father fried fish on a school night, the aroma wafting through their tiny flat. When fish was being cooked, Orko's homework was sketchy, full of little mistakes that his teacher would later mark in red ink scrawled over his own handwriting. They ate the curry with little rice – the whole point of the meal was the fish. When they finished, there were mounds of fish bones by the sides of their plates. They sat there long after they had finished eating, the flavour of the fish seeping into them through their tongues, their nostrils, the tips of their fingers. Back when Orko loved fish, he told his father everything – the mischief that he got up to with his friends; the colour of his history teacher's saree; the contents of Urmi's tiffin box, and the fact that Urmi herself got to eat very little of it. Nandan interjected at times, with a comment or a question.

Now they sit silently at the table with the three chairs around it. Just as Orko is about to excuse himself, his father clears his throat as if he's going to say something. The curry is drying on Orko's fingers, and he knows that the smell is going to linger through the night, even if he rinses his mouth with toothpaste and washes his hands with detergent.

'Is everything all right?' Nandan asks tentatively.

The words trigger a series of sensations in Orko's body. At first it's just between his eyes, at the top of the bridge of his nose. At this point, he still can taste the fish curry on his palate. Then it grows to fill the region between his ears, until they're burning. It flows down his gullet and fills his windpipe. He finds it difficult to breathe. It reaches his fingertips, and he feels them shake. It fills his stomach until he feels like he might vomit, right here, at the dining table. It travels to his loins, and down his femurs. He wants to go to the bathroom but his muscles won't obey. He feels like throwing his plate against the wall but he can't move a muscle. He can't do anything at all.

He doesn't want to cry, but the twitch in his stomach grows into sobs, and soon, in spite of himself, he is weeping, retching, banging his head on the table. He hears his father's chair fall over. He can't stand being touched, but he doesn't want to hurt his father's feelings.

'Tell me what's wrong. You can tell me anything. Anything at all.'

This is when Orko realises that he is angry. He wishes his father had said these words months ago, when he came home after afternoons with Bishu and ate his dinner in silence. Now they're just words. Impotent. Hollow. Sentences devoid of import.

He walks past his father to the sink in the kitchen. He remembers the plates, with the little hillocks of fish bones by their sides. His father is still standing by the dining table, dumbstruck. Orko gathers the plates and carries them off to the kitchen. His fingers tremble as he brushes the fish bones into the garbage can. He rinses the plates and stacks them under the sink. He reaches for the bar of soap on the shelf by the sink, but it has reduced to a disgusting puddle of green goo that he doesn't want to touch.

In the living room he finds Nandan in his armchair, lost in thought. Orko hurries past, eyes downcast.

'You can talk to me, you know,' says his father. 'I'm not a stranger, after all. I've also been through adolescence. I have, perhaps, felt many of the things you're feeling now. Maybe it'll help to just talk.'

'You're the one who said that I should never speak when I'm angry,' Orko replies from the threshold of his bedroom. 'Besides, it's late.'

He shuts the door behind him. Inside, it's dark. The grille on his window, with its unimaginative pattern of rectangles, is reborn in the fluorescent light from the neighbouring block of flats. He switches on the fan and lies down, staring as the blades slice through the shadows, ripping them to shreds.

There's a knock on his door.

'Leave me alone,' he says.

His father comes in anyway.

'Go away, please!' Orko begs.

Nandan does not go away. He sits, silently, by Orko's side. Orko turns over to lie on his stomach, burying his face in his pillow. His body begins to tremble. He bites his pillow, willing himself to be still.

'It isn't easy,' his father says. 'It is perfectly okay to feel the way you're feeling.'

'You don't know how I'm feeling,' Orko retorts. 'You couldn't possibly...'

Nandan runs his fingers through Orko's hair. 'When I was your age, I would become angry about a lot of things. Angry about all the rules I had to follow. Angry that I had to study engineering. Angry that I couldn't go to the movies like my friends did. Angry at the stupidity of the people around me. Angry, just because.'

This is impossible for Orko to imagine. He suspects that his father is just saying all of this to make him feel better.

'It's important, after the anger dies down, to figure out exactly what it was that made you angry,' Nandan continues.

'You don't actually understand how I feel,' says Orko. 'You just want to lecture me.'

Nandan lets out a chuckle. 'You remind me of your mother. She would become angry for no apparent reason. She would throw things, shout at me, call me names. When she calmed down she would be remorseful, but she wouldn't be able to say why she had been angry.'

'Please go away,' says Orko. This time he's not pleading. The tone of his own voice frightens him.

Nandan sighs, and takes Orko's hand in his. 'Know that I am here for you. You can tell me anything at all. When you feel better, let's try to understand what it is that is bothering you.'

He sets a book down by Orko's pillow.

'You haven't been reading much these past few weeks. Read this book. I read it when I was your age, and I now realise that it was one of the most instructive books I read as a boy.'

After his father leaves the room, Orko holds up the book so the light from the window falls on its jacket. It's Maugham. His anger is now unbearable, and it isn't because his father doesn't know that he has already read this book. It is because Orko didn't find it instructive at all.

Ten

Orko is late for school. The last time he was late, it was because there had been an accident at the foot of the Dhakuria bridge, and the traffic had come to a standstill. He had walked the rest of the way to school, getting there just as assembly was coming to an end. He had to go to the administrator's office and explain why he was late.

Today he's late because he waited outside the school gates, out of sight of the guard, until he heard the chorus of the school anthem. The guard waves him through. Orko runs past the playground and catches up with his classmates at the foot of the stairs that lead up to the classrooms. Brishti greets him; Orko merely nods an acknowledgement. Nilanjana asks him why he wasn't at assembly, and he tells her that he overslept. When they reach their floor, Orko inserts himself between Brishti and Nilanjana. He is hyper-alert as they walk past Kaushik's classroom, although he doesn't really know what he would do if Kaushik and Pratik were to accost him again.

The hours are unendingly long, and his teachers seem to be speaking a language that he's only vaguely familiar with. He understands the individual sentences, but not how they go together. He doesn't speak with anyone. Brishti glances towards him more than a few times, but he avoids making eye contact. He studies Paromita out of the corner of his eye, but he can't tell if she knows what happened by the guava tree. He wonders if she would be upset with Kaushik if she found out.

When the lunch bell rings, he remembers that he left his tiffin box in the schoolyard, by the guava tree. It would probably be at the lost property office downstairs, but to get there he would have to go past Kaushik's classroom. He sits quietly at his desk as his classmates disperse for their walks around the playground. He really needs to go to the bathroom, and now seems like a good time to go. Kaushik is probably downstairs by the swings, but Orko can't be sure that he hasn't told the other boys. He doesn't want to run into somebody else who's going to call him names. Just as he's on the verge of going anyway, Brishti thrusts her open tiffin box to his side of their desk.

'I'm not hungry,' he says.

'Come over to my place after school, then? We'll have lunch together?'

'I have to go home,' Orko replies, although that isn't strictly true.

'Please? I hate having lunch by myself.'

Orko doesn't know what to think. They've shared a desk for months now, and this is the first time she has asked him to lunch.

'Okay,' he says, before rushing off to the toilet. His lower abdomen hurts, and he's afraid he is going to wet his pants if he waits any longer.

'Here we are,' Brishti says as they come to a two-storey house in a cul-de-sac about half a kilometre from their school. It is a large house, lime-green, with purple bougainvillea running along the boundary wall. The windows and the front gate are also green, although a shade darker. Brishti unlatches the gate and walks up the steps to the front balcony. She presses a white button by the door. The doorbell sounds like the horn of a scooter, far away. They wait at the doorstep in an awkward silence.

The woman who answers the door is dressed in a red saree that has seen neither starch nor iron. Her hair is in a neat, shiny bun.

'Komola-mashi, this is Orko. He's going to have lunch with me today,' Brishti tells the woman as she shuts and latches the door behind them. This is the first time Orko has heard Brishti speak Bangla; she speaks it as if it were a foreign language.

Komola-mashi smiles at Orko. 'Would you like something to drink before lunch?' she asks them. 'Lemonade? A glass of cold water?'

'I'd like some water, please,' Orko says after some hesitation. His throat is parched.

The room is sparsely furnished. There is a bookshelf along the wall to their right. On the bookshelf is a telephone. It's a black rotary instrument, like the one in his grandfather's house. He remembers trying to lift it as a child, and finding it too heavy. 'Bakelite,' his grandfather had said when Orko asked him what it was made of. Orko found the name very odd, because the phone was not light at all.

There's a set of rattan chairs around a low, round table, with the newspaper and a few periodicals arranged neatly on its glass surface. The newspaper is weighed down by a brass ashtray in the shape of a goblin's shoe. At the centre of the table is a glass cup, filled halfway with marbles – blue, green, cat's eye.

'Sit down, sit down,' says Brishti. She turns on the ceiling fan. It is a vintage model, with four blades around an ornate hub. It stirs to life with surprising alacrity, gathering speed with the grace of a dervish.

Komola-mashi returns with two glasses of water on a wooden tray. 'Don't you want to shower before lunch?' she asks Brishti.

Brishti glances at Orko. 'A quick one today,' she says. 'We're both very hungry.'

Orko wonders how Brishti knows he's hungry. He wishes he could shower too, but he hasn't brought a change of clothes with him.

'Do you want to freshen up?' Brishti asks him.

'I'm fine,' he says. 'Maybe I'll just wash my face and hands.'

'Come with me,' Brishti says, and Orko sets his empty glass down on the coffee table.

They pass through a doorway and into a large room. There's a six-seat dining table to their left. They go past it, into a narrow passageway. At the end is an iron grille of indeterminate colour, with a patch of grass beyond it. To their left is a staircase, and to their right a large door, its varnished surface polished to a shine.

'Here,' says Brishti, pushing the door open. 'I think the towel's fresh. I'll be back in a jiffy.' Orko waits until she is halfway up the stairs before he enters the bathroom and shuts the door behind him.

The bathroom is about half the size of his bedroom, with a fan hanging from the ceiling. Orko has never been in a bathroom with a ceiling fan. The commode, the cistern and the washbasin are brilliant white porcelain. The washbasin has separate taps for hot and cold water.

Orko undoes his trousers and lets them drop to his ankles. He sits on the commode, and continues to sit there long after he has relieved himself. If he had a bathroom like this, he would put in a bookshelf and a stereo, and he would spend hours in there reading, the ceiling fan whirring overhead. He has spent many hours of his life in bathrooms. His grandmother once took him to a homeopathic doctor because he went so often, spending close to an hour each time. He took the newspaper with him, or a magazine, or, if he was lucky enough to find one lying around, a book of short stories. He never took novels to the bathroom. Orko didn't tell the doctor that he spent so much time in the bathroom because he liked to be alone, because surely that couldn't be a disease. Besides, he really liked homeopathic medicines – those tiny white globules, sickly sweet, moistened with alcohol. Dr Sinha concluded that Orko had an irritable bowel and wrote out a prescription in his indecipherable hand.

A lizard clicks, four times, and it sounds like it is right behind Orko. He whirls around, but there's no lizard to be found. He stands reluctantly and pulls his trousers up from around his ankles. He looks at his reflection in the large mirror over the washbasin. His shirt is surprisingly clean, with just a faint hint of perspiration around the armpits. There's a soap dispenser by the tap. Orko squeezes out a puddle into the cup of his right hand. He works up a lather and scrubs his face. He lathers his hands and his arms, right up to the elbows. He washes his face and his arms until they no longer feel soapy. He wipes himself dry with the towel that hangs by the washbasin. The towel smells of an unfamiliar detergent.

When he emerges from the bathroom, Brishti is at the foot of the stairs. She is dressed in light cotton trousers with a floral print, and a faded shirt that's just a shade lighter than peach. Orko wishes he had clothes like Brishti's. A familiar envy comes over him; he tries to shake it off, and is embarrassed when he realises that he is actually shaking his head from side to side.

'What is it?' Brishti asks.

'Nothing,' says Orko.

'I'm starving,' she says. 'Shall we eat?'

'Well, I'm a little hungry myself,' Orko says. He can feel his stomach rumble.

The table has already been laid, with two places set side by side. Brishti switches on the ceiling fan. Orko looks up just as it swishes to life. This one is a utilitarian model: white, three blades.

Brishti pulls out the chair that's closest to the head of the table. Orko sits to her right. Opposite them is a sideboard, polished to a shine. It has a stack of drawers to the left and a glass door to the right. Behind the glass door are china plates, a large teapot with matching cups and saucers, and an assortment of glasses. Some of the glasses are ordinary. Some look like cups sitting on long stalks. Orko has seen glasses like them in old black-and-white movies.

Komola-mashi serves Orko first, heaping on ladles of rice until he holds out his hand over the plate.

'What's that?' she says with a smile. 'You're a growing boy. It won't do to eat so little!' She moves to Brishti's plate, and when she's done, Orko notices that the heap of rice is smaller than the one on his own.

'It's nothing special,' says Brishti. 'Just everyday stuff.'

They eat quickly, silently, and before long their plates are empty, the curry drying on their fingers. Orko waits for Brishti to finish washing her hands before rising from his seat. He wonders if he should rinse his plate, like he does at home. He decides against it; when he had lunch with Urmi, her mother forbade him to rinse his plate.

The staircase is wide, the steps yellow mosaic. The banister is black, its concrete surface cold to the touch. At the top of the stairs is a hall, bathed in sunlight streaming through two sets of skylights in the ceiling. They pass beneath the skylights and through a door at the far end of the hall, into a room that's a little larger than Orko's. The walls look like they've been painted recently. They're peach, a few shades darker than Brishti's shirt. To the left is a bunk bed that reminds Orko of an illustration from a book he read as a child. Along the wall adjoining the bed is an armoire and a chest of drawers, the varnish on them so fresh he can smell it. Beside the chest is a bookshelf, but most of the shelf space is taken up by records. There's a stereo on a shelf halfway from the top. Opposite the bed is a set of French windows, opening onto a balcony. In the corner by the window is an upright piano, with a stool that looks much older than the piano.

'You play the piano?' Orko asks, surprised. They've had many conversations about music, and Brishti hasn't mentioned that she plays an instrument.

'Sort of,' she says. 'My mother has a piano. I missed it after we moved here. I've only had this one for a few weeks.'

There isn't a desk in the room, and there aren't any chairs. Orko turns his attention to the bunk bed. The lower berth is unremarkable. A pillow; a neatly folded duvet by the footboard; a paperback book, face-down, by the pillow. A ladder with five rungs is affixed to the lip of the upper berth. Upstairs is a table, about a foot and a half in height. On the table is a pencil stand, a history textbook and a couple of notebooks. There are three cushions along the wall, and a duvet, moss green, in a heap by the headboard.

'Sit,' says Brishti, and Orko is reminded of a song in which a girl asks the singer to sit, but there's no chair in her room. There's a rug in the song, but there isn't one here. Orko sits gingerly on the edge of the bed. Brishti chuckles. 'It's not a toy bed, you know,' she says, handing him a cushion. 'Sit comfortably. It won't break.'

Orko props the cushion up against the wall. He lifts his feet onto the surface of the bed. His heels look filthy and cracked. He quickly puts his feet back on the ground.

'Have you read this?' Brishti asks as she hands him a book. *The History of Middle-earth*, it says on the cover. She throws a pillow against the headboard. She sits cross-legged, an arm's distance from Orko. Her heels are smooth and clean.

Orko hasn't read the book. 'You can take it home with you,' Brishti says. They talk about the world of J.R.R. Tolkien, about Lothlórien, about Tinúviel and Aragorn, and soon the state of Orko's heels seems insignificant. He leans against the wall and stretches his legs out in front of him. There's a lull in the conversation. A radio plays in the distance. Orko catches the chief minister's name. It's a newscast.

Sitting here, on the lower berth of the bunk bed, Orko feels as if he's in a room within a room, like Urmi's doll's house, the one whose roof came off so they could arrange the furniture inside. As a child, he would often lie in bed, daydreaming, imagining himself inside that house, with the kitchen all around him, life-size. The blue three-legged table at the centre, the stove by the window, the saucepan on the stove, the giant teapot on the floor.

'Something happened to you yesterday,' says Brishti, drawing Orko out of his reverie.

'What?' Orko asks, startled. 'What happened? How do you know?'

'You didn't come back after lunch,' says Brishti, 'and you've been preoccupied all day. I saw you doodling in your notebooks instead of taking notes.'

Orko hadn't imagined that he would tell anyone about his encounter with Kaushik. He tries to piece together the narrative in a series of short, coherent sentences, but he doesn't know where to begin, so he skips right to the end. 'Kaushik and Pratik jumped me in the schoolyard,' he says.

'Just like that?' Brishti asks, incredulous.

Orko shrugs. He wants to tell Brishti everything, but he dithers, worrying that she too will think he is a pervert. He doesn't think that she would, but he can't be sure.

'Do you think I'm weird?' he asks, in a manner that suggests that he doesn't really care either way.

Brishti looks at him intently, as if she's trying to decide how to answer his question. 'Yes, you're a little weird,' she says, just as Orko is beginning to think she isn't going to respond. 'I had a friend who was a lot like you.'

'How do you mean?' Orko asks.

'Well, he was a very sweet boy, for one,' says Brishti. 'And he didn't really get along with the rest of the boys.'

'I have no problem with boys,' Orko retorts. 'I used to play football with a whole bunch of them.'

'He had a crush on Tom Cruise,' Brishti says. She has a faraway look in her eyes, and Orko gathers, from the tone of her voice, that the story did not end very well for this friend.

'I don't have a crush on anyone,' he says defiantly.

'I overheard your conversation the other day,' Brishti says. 'You were talking about one of our teachers.' She's smiling, and she doesn't look like she thinks Orko is a deviant.

'I just said he was cute,' Orko says. 'I don't have a crush on him or anything like that.'

'Have you ever wanted to kiss a boy?' she asks casually, as if she were asking him if he liked strawberries, or if he had ever seen a vulture.

Orko's first instinct is to feign disgust, but he's tired of lying, hiding, pretending. Her question is simple enough, but the answer is less so. He thinks about Priya and the bearded man kissing, but that image is quickly replaced by another: Bishu's moustache brushing against his upper lip; Bishu's fingers pressing so hard against his cheeks that his jaws came unclenched; Bishu's tongue, like sandpaper, thrusting into his mouth; a sensation not unlike drowning as Bishu's breath, all garlic and cigarettes, mingled with his own. 'This is what you do before you fuck a woman,' Bishu had said by way of explanation.

'What happened to your friend?' he asks, in an effort to change the topic.

'They said he had an accident,' says Brishti. 'I don't believe it for a moment, though.'

'What, then?'

'I think he took his own life.'

When a new acquaintance asks Orko about his parents, he tells them that he lives with his father, and that his mother is dead, and they usually express regret. If anybody other than Brishti had told him about a friend who died, Orko would probably say that he was sorry it happened. With Brishti, though, that doesn't seem necessary, or appropriate, because when he told her that his mother had died, she merely said that she missed her mother too, and she wished she could speak to her more often.

'What was his name?' he asks.

'Joshua,' says Brishti. 'Josh.'

'Do you have a picture?'

Brishti fetches a photo album, mustard-yellow, from the top drawer of the chest. She sits down beside him, their shoulders so close that they're almost touching. She opens the album near its middle. She flips a page, then another. 'That's him,' she says.

The picture seems to have been taken on a basketball court, although none of the people in it is dressed for basketball. Brishti looks very different in the photograph. Her hair is longer, and she isn't wearing spectacles. The girl to her left is shorter than her, her hair so fair that it's almost white. Josh is to Brishti's right. He is about as tall as Brishti, which would make him an inch or two shorter than Orko. They're all smiling at the camera.

From the picture, Orko would never have imagined that Josh would take his own life. His wispy brown hair ends at his collar. He has sharp features, and wide, almond eyes. Orko struggles to find an adjective to describe him. He would settle on 'pretty', but he knows that when a boy is called pretty, it isn't a compliment.

When Orko reaches home, dusk is beginning to fall. He switches on the lights in the stairwell. The weariness of the past few days seems to have left him, and he takes the steps two, three at a time. He can hear his neighbour's television set as he fumbles with his keys. He leaves the door ajar and makes his way to the light switch by the refrigerator. He toggles the switch but nothing happens. He tries the ceiling fan, with the same result.

He goes back down the stairs, not knowing what he should do. There's a bank of fuse boxes and power meters beneath the staircase, but staring at them is not going to help him diagnose the problem. Feeling woefully inadequate, he heads to the caretaker's quarters at the back of the compound.

'A man from the electric company was here,' Kedar-dada says apologetically. 'He said that your bill hasn't been paid for six months. I told him there must be a mistake, and that I would tell Sengupta-babu to get in touch with him, but he wouldn't listen.'

At first Orko can't believe that his father could forget to pay the bill for six consecutive months. On the first Sunday of every month, Nandan sits at their dining table with his diary, writing out cheques for their monthly bills and enclosing cash in envelopes for the milkman and the paperboy. Orko tries to recall the last time he saw his father at this monthly ritual, but he can't.

For the first time in his life, Orko is worried about his father. There was a time when Nandan would say that eating out frequently was terrible for one's health. Now, more often than not, they have dinner at a dingy little Chinese restaurant near the bus terminus. Sometimes Nandan doesn't even feel like walking the five minutes that it takes them to get there. He sends Orko to a grimy roadside stall for chicken curry and roti. Sometimes Nandan doesn't come home for dinner, and Orko eats toast and eggs, saving the takeout money for himself.

Back in the flat, Orko lights a candle. He lets a few drops of wax fall onto the surface of an old saucer. He presses the bottom of the candle into the puddle of wax, waiting for it to cool. The flat looks eerily different in candlelight. The walls seem to recede, making the living room appear much larger than it is. He sets a cushion against an armrest and lies on the sofa. On the ceiling, the fan casts a shadow that looks like an alien spacecraft. The cushions on the sofa look brown, although he knows that they're green. The refrigerator, sky-blue, is now an indeterminate colour. On the refrigerator is the familiar photo frame, but his mother's image is lost in the shadows.

When Brishti showed him Joshua's photo, Orko was reminded of his mother glancing sideways at him from the top of the refrigerator. On his way back from Brishti's, he surmised that this was because they were both beautiful, and because neither of them would ever be old and infirm. Now he realises that they have another thing in common: the manner of their deaths was shrouded in secrecy. No one ever talked about his mother's passing; when he asked questions, he was always told that his mother's heart had stopped beating. This frustrated him, because ultimately everybody died because their hearts stopped beating. Finally, an answer begins to emerge from the shadows of the years. It begins to seem very likely that his mother, like Joshua, had taken her own life.

Eleven

After the incident by the guava tree, Orko stopped going to the schoolyard by himself, and he avoided going to the bathrooms on their floor, lest he run into Kaushik. For the first few days, he became angry and resentful when he thought about the situation. Weeks passed, then months, and now it seems as though this is how things always were. He is always vigilant, and he doesn't indulge in frivolities such as walks in the schoolyard with his classmates. In the morning, he waits outside the gates until he hears the bell for assembly. He falls in line at the last moment, and he stays close to Brishti and Nilanjana when they make their way to their classroom. He spends the break indoors, with Brishti. After school, he usually goes to Brishti's house and has lunch with her.

It begins to rain just as Orko and Brishti leave school. It's just a few drops in the beginning, so they keep going, but it's pouring by the time they've walked half the way to Brishti's house. Orko breaks into a run. Brishti keeps her composure for a while, walking briskly, holding her bag up to cover her head. Then she too begins to run. By the time they reach her house, they're both drenched. They giggle as Brishti fires off a volley of buzzes on the doorbell.

'Oh my! Look at the two of you,' Komola-mashi exclaims. 'Are you crazy? Couldn't you have stopped for shelter? You're going to fall ill!'

Orko is glad to be indoors. He is drenched to the bone. He's worried that his books are soaking wet, as is the change of clothes he's carrying in his schoolbag. For a moment he considers going back home. There's a thunderclap, deafeningly loud.

'Wait here,' Komola-mashi says. 'I'll bring you some towels.'

They wait as instructed, dripping pools of water on the shiny mosaic floor. Orko shrugs off his schoolbag and undoes the clasps. His change of clothes is damp. The ink on the labels of his notebooks has begun to run.

'It's all wet,' he says in despair. 'I had better head home. Is there a raincoat or an umbrella that I can borrow?'

'Don't be an idiot,' Brishti retorts. 'You'll catch your death of cold. Your books will be pulp by the time you get home.'

Komola-mashi rushes in with an armload of towels. Brishti takes one and wipes herself down vigorously. Orko gingerly pats himself dry.

'Dry your hair,' Komola-mashi says to him, before turning to Brishti. 'Why don't you give him some of your father's clothes?'

Brishti grabs him by the arm. 'Let's go,' she says. 'I think I can lend you a T-shirt and a pair of trousers.'

'You should both have a hot shower,' Komola-mashi calls after them. 'I've switched on the water heaters in the bathrooms upstairs.'

They make their way to the staircase.

'Take your shoes off – you're tracking mud all over the floor,' Komola-mashi complains. The floor is covered in muddy boot prints.

Orko is ashamed. He would never be so careless in his own home. If his shoes were muddy, he would take them off before he walked through the front door.

As he follows Brishti up the stairway, Orko has an uncanny sense of having done exactly this before. It's not quite deja vu, but it's close. He has a shadowy memory of being ten years old and drenched to the bone, following Urmi up the stairs to her flat.

'I'll bring you some clothes,' Brishti says when they're at the top of the stairs.

It seems strange to Orko that although he has been to Brishti's more than a hundred times now, he is yet to meet her father. The only other friend that he has visited so many times is Urmi, and her parents are like a second family to him. Even now, he sometimes goes to their flat just to say hello to them. Brishti's father, on the other hand, is an enigma. She has shown him a picture, taken many years ago. She speaks of her mother often, but never of her father. Sometimes it seems to him that Brishti doesn't want him to meet her father. He felt that way a few times early on in their friendship, but he had dismissed the feeling as a figment of his imagination. It was only about a month ago that he began to believe it.

It was a Saturday. They had been assigned a lot of homework that week, and Orko hadn't being paying attention during their economics lessons. He rang Brishti to ask her if he could come over after lunch. He had been to Brishti's house only a couple of times that week, so he thought that she would welcome the idea.

'Why don't we compare notes on Monday,' she said, under her breath. Usually, their phone conversations lasted at least a few minutes, but that morning she hung up promptly. Orko pictured her glancing furtively over her shoulder as they exchanged the rushed sentences.

Just the other day, they had been listening to music, and had lost track of time. When Komola-mashi brought them tea and samosas, it was dark outside.

'Look at the time!' Brishti exclaimed. 'Why didn't you tell me it was past six?'

As they sipped their tea, Brishti began to seem increasingly anxious. She ate her samosas in uncharacteristically large bites. When Orko took his time, she glared at him admonishingly. She closed Orko's notebooks and stacked up all his belongings in a neat pile. In the end, she looked like she might begin to cry. Orko left his samosa half-eaten. He packed his belongings and left as soon as he could. He wondered, then, if she was ashamed of being friends with him.

'Here,' says Brishti, handing him a set of clothes bundled in a blue towel. 'I think they'll fit you. Use my bathroom – I'll use the other one.' She motions towards her father's room.

In the bathroom, Orko struggles to extricate himself from his sodden clothes. They seem to have shrunk around his body. His skin feels cold and clammy. He turns on the tap and steps under the shower. The water is cold at first, then lukewarm, and finally scalding hot. He fiddles with the taps on the shower column until the temperature is just right. Orko rarely uses a shower. Nandan had once told him that showering for five minutes wasted twenty buckets of water.

At home he bathes with a bucket and a mug, never using more than two buckets of water.

As he dries himself, Orko notices the clothes that Brishti has given him. He recognises the pastel blue trousers and the white cotton shirt – they're Brishti's. She was right. They do fit him perfectly, except that the trousers are just a little shorter than he would have liked. The shirt buttons are on the wrong side, and the collar is narrow and curved. The floral print looks like it has been pencilled in. The trousers are of a light material, softer than any he has worn. When he sees himself in the mirror, he is startled; this is the least ugly he has felt in a very long time. He uses his fingers to comb his hair.

When Orko comes out of the bathroom, Brishti is back after her shower. She smiles at him. She looks like she's about to say something, but she doesn't.

'What?' Orko demands. He's almost certain it's going to be a jibe about the clothes.

'Nothing,' says Brishti.

'No, you were about to say something,' Orko insists.

'Just that you're looking pretty,' says Brishti, with a twinkle in her eye.

Orko has been called pretty before – in the boys' bathrooms at school, in the changing rooms at the swimming club, on the football field – and it has always been a taunt, usually followed by a pinch on his buttocks or a punch to his stomach. This time, though, it's different. Brishti is still smiling, and Orko can't detect even the faintest whiff of derision in her expression.

'Lunch?' she asks, and heads out without waiting for Orko to respond.

Downstairs, Komola-mashi is ready for them. 'You two look like twins,' she says. 'Sit down. The food's getting cold.' It's true; they really do look like twins, dressed in slacks and shirts, their wet hair slicked back, their earlobes bare.

The rice is piping hot, the chicken curry delicious. They eat quietly, ravenously. Halfway through the meal, Orko begins to feel a little bit anxious.

'Do you have an iron?' he asks Brishti.

'What do you want with an iron?' Brishti asks, surprised.

'I have to dry my clothes. I can't possibly go home in these,' he says, regretting the words the moment they escape his lips. What if Brishti thought he didn't like her clothes?

'Don't worry. I won't miss them,' Brishti says as she gets up from the table.

They wash their hands and head back upstairs to Brishti's room.

'I know you won't miss them,' Orko says. 'It's just that...'

Brishti cuts him off. 'You're looking nice,' she says. 'Really.'

Orko hesitates. 'People are going to stare,' he says.

'Stare back at them,' Brishti says. 'That's the first thing I learned after I moved here. People stare at me all the time, as if I'm a monkey in a zoo. The only thing to do is stare right back.'

They sit on the lower berth of the bunk bed, side by side. Orko wishes he didn't have to go home today. Brishti's room is cosy and warm. Outside, the rain beats against the windowpanes and on umbrellas turned inside out by the wind.

'I don't think we can do our homework now,' Orko says. 'My books are all wet.'

'So are mine,' says Brishti. 'Scrabble?'

'Sure,' says Orko.

After they've played a few turns, the board resembles an incomplete crossword puzzle. Orko shuffles the tiles around on the bench, sure that he can use all seven tiles for his next turn, if only he can find an opening.

'Do you like *The Sound of Music*?' Brishti asks.

'Yes, of course,' he says. 'I watched it with my mother. That was the first time I went to the cinema.'

'Wait till you hear this, then,' she says, and walks over to the shelves by the stereo. She stands on her toes and picks out a record, without really looking. She raises the lid of the turntable. She fishes the shiny black disc out of its well-worn jacket and places it on the platter. 'It's one of my favourites,' she says. 'The record actually belongs to my mother,' she adds, closing the lid softly.

There's a faint crackling, followed by a few bars of piano. Then a wind instrument plays the first few notes of 'My Favourite Things'.

Brishti potters about, emptying her schoolbag and laying out its damp contents on the floor. Orko wishes she would stop.

'Do you like it?' Brishti asks when the song is over.

'It's amazing,' Orko says.

'Do you think this music would exist if all anyone could do was to sing the song the way it was written, words and all?' Brishti asks.

The record plays on, and Orko is a little embarrassed because he can't recognise the instrument. The songs are long, and they don't seem to have any discernible structure. It's almost as if the musicians are just playing like children in a playground, and the music is an accident.

'Don't you sometimes wish that you were like everybody else?' Brishti asks, just as the record comes to an end.

'What do you mean?' Orko retorts, trying to appear less anxious than he feels.

Brishti doesn't seem to have heard him. She fidgets with the tassels of the bedcover.

'I'm here because I'm not like everybody else,' she says. 'If I was, I would be home, in Montreal, and I could see my mother whenever I wanted. I don't even have friends here.'

Orko feels a twinge of sadness, because he thinks of Brishti as his closest friend now. 'Do you have many friends back home?' he asks.

'Not many,' Brishti says. 'But I do have a few people that I'm really close to.' She retrieves a diary from the top shelf of the record cabinet. She flips through its pages and brings out a photograph. It's a polaroid. Orko's uncle has a polaroid camera, and Orko had been wonderstruck to see his own likeness printed out on the little square just minutes after his uncle pressed the shutter. Brishti is in this photograph. She's standing behind a girl with long golden hair. Orko remembers seeing her in the picture with Joshua, on the basketball court. In this picture Brishti has her arms around her.

'That's Janice,' she says.

'She looks like Tinúviel,' says Orko.

Brishti laughs out loud. 'You had better not say that to her face,' she says. 'She hates *The Lord of the Rings*.'

Orko doesn't have photographs of any of his friends. But then, the only real friend he's had lives within shouting distance of his home. He can't fathom how Brishti must feel about being so far away from her mother, and from her friends. It seems really cruel of her father to have moved her to Calcutta.

'You must be really close to her,' he says.

'She's the reason I'm here,' says Brishti.

Orko is intrigued. 'I don't understand,' he says.

Brishti looks at the photograph for a long time, then replaces it between the pages of her diary. 'I tell my mother everything,' she says.

'Yeah, I used to do that too,' he says.

'Did you ever regret it?' Brishti asks.

Orko remembers that time by the swimming pool, when he told his mother that he hated being a boy. He remembers her heart beating against his as she held him. That is his last tactile memory of her, because it was shortly afterwards that she disappeared.

'Yes,' he says. 'There are a few things that I shouldn't have told her.'

'My mother knows everything about me,' Brishti says. 'I just wish she hadn't told my father.'

It is immediately clear to Orko that he has been confided in, but it takes him a while to fully comprehend the essence of what he has been told. He struggles to respond. 'You mean...Janice...'

Brishti smiles. 'My mother asked me if I had a boy-friend,' she says. 'And I said I did, but my boyfriend was a girl.'

'And then?' Orko asks, his thoughts in disarray, like pieces of a jigsaw puzzle scattered on the floor.

'She said I was too young to have boyfriends, or girlfriends for that matter...but she also said that Janice seemed like a sweet girl.'

'And your father?' Orko asks.

'He went ballistic,' says Brishti.

She doesn't elaborate on the shenanigans that followed, but Orko can't imagine that the process of moving halfway across the world could have come about without conflict or confrontation. He begins to understand why Brishti doesn't want him to meet her father.

'Well,' he says, pausing to choose his words. 'If I was a girl, I too would probably have a boyfriend who was a girl.'

'But you're a boy,' says Brishti. 'And maybe you'll have a boyfriend, when you're older.'

Brishti is obviously alluding to the conversation with Paromita and Nilanjana. Orko isn't sure that he would like to have a boyfriend. He can't dismiss the idea entirely, but he doesn't want to give Brishti the wrong impression. 'Having a crush isn't quite the same as having a boyfriend,' he says. 'Boys are stupid. If I had a boyfriend, it would take us five minutes to run out of conversation.'

Brishti doesn't respond to this. Orko glances at her, but she's fidgeting with the tassels again, a faraway look in her eyes. 'I've always wished I was a girl,' he says absent-mindedly. He's surprised by the way the words sound, because this is the first time he has said them out aloud.

'Why do you wish that you were a girl?' she asks.

Orko has asked himself this question many times, and he never has been able arrive at a satisfactory answer.

'I just hate being so alone,' he begins. 'I can't hang around with the boys. They're horrid, except for maybe one or two of them. I don't want to talk about cricket, or kung-fu, or Bollywood actresses. It's completely inane.'

'So you don't have to,' Brishti says. 'You can choose your friends. There aren't any boys in our class.'

Orko struggles to respond. It is easier said than done. He thinks about the sleepovers he's never invited to, and the conversations that die the moment he appears. 'It's so hard,' he begins.

Brishti cuts him short. 'Have you ever wondered why I haven't been to your house yet? It's because I'm not allowed to. I have to come straight home from school. I can't be out after dark. I can't wear the skirt my mother wore when she was my age. It's all for my own safety – that's what I'm told. I was eight years old when my mother told me that I should be wary of strange men, because of what they might do to me.' Orko has never seen Brishti become as angry as she seems now.

'So are you saying you'd rather be a boy?' he asks, tentatively.

'Of course not,' she says. 'I don't like boys either. You're my friend only because you're not like the rest of them.'

'What do you mean?'

'They act as if they're the kings of the world. They're constantly sizing you up, assigning you a score based on how pretty you are.'

Orko knows this is true, from conversations he's overheard at the football field, in the boys' bathrooms at school and in other places where there are no girls within earshot. He wonders what Brishti would say if she knew that the boys also talk about breast sizes of naked women in magazines, and that they squabble about who among them has the biggest penis.

'Ever since I moved here it's been horrible,' she goes on. 'On the street, men my father's age leer at me. Boys follow me, telling each other crude jokes, loudly, so I can hear them. The one time that I tried taking the bus, a man kept brushing his arm against my breast as I stood by the door trying to elbow my way in.'

Orko knows every word Brishti is saying is true, because some of it has happened to him too, only it didn't happen to him because he was a girl. It happened to him because he was weird. When he remembered to walk like Bishu taught him, the boys didn't laugh at him or pass lewd comments. When he stuck his elbows out in the bus, taking up more space than he needed, no one made a grab for his crotch. When he grows up, grows a beard and dresses like his father, no one will harass him in buses and on footpaths and at bus stops. Brishti – and Urmi, and Nilanjana, and even Paromita – will have to put up with it for as long as they live. He feels numb. 'It has stopped raining,' he says. 'I had better get home before it starts up again.'

He's a few metres from the bus stop when he hears the familiar booming voice calling his name. At first he thinks his mind is playing tricks on him, and he hurries on. Then he hears the voice again. He resists the urge to whirl around and ascertain that it really is Bishu, here, at the bus stop that he waits at every day. He breaks into a run.

He leaves the bus stop behind, picking up his pace as a visceral terror threatens to paralyse him. He ducks into a lane, just past the foot of the bridge, taking turns at random until he begins to suspect that he's going around in circles. Completely out of breath, he sits on the edge of the footpath, hugging his knees to keep his insides from heaving. When the terror begins to subside, he realises he is hopelessly lost.

Twelve

On the way to school, the bus is more crowded than usual – it's standing room only. Orko hangs on to the overhead rail with both hands. The man seated directly in front of him offers to hold Orko's schoolbag. Orko slips it off his shoulders and smiles at the man, to thank him for his kindness. The ride seems interminably long. When they're at a traffic signal, Orko takes one hand off the rail to check his trouser pocket. The money's still there.

It is a lot of money. When Orko retrieved the biscuit tin from the back of his cupboard yesterday, he was surprised; there was seven hundred rupees in the box. When he was counting the money it had merely been an idle exercise; he wasn't thinking about the things that he could do with it. Now he speculates about the prices of train tickets to destinations as far away as he dares to imagine. Cochin. Trivandrum. Madras. He finally settles on Dehradun, because his aunt used to live there, and she once told him that there was a hill station close by, where the snow came down like wisps of cotton.

They move in fits and starts, and the going is so slow that Orko wonders if he would be better off walking the rest of the way. A woman steps off the footpath and hails an auto-rickshaw. She has two large shopping bags on her arm. She pulls the straps up to her shoulder with a quick flick of her wrist. Orko surmises that she's on her way to

Gariahat market. When he went to the market with his father, they usually spent more than three hundred rupees on the fish and the vegetables they bought for the week. When Nandan bought *hilsa*, or prawns, or mutton, it was closer to five hundred rupees. He fingers the notes in his pocket, growing anxious that it isn't enough money. Perhaps he can avoid buying a ticket altogether. He could find a seat in an unreserved compartment and hide in the toilet when the ticket examiner came. Or maybe he could just say that he had no ticket, and no money. He would be forced to disembark at a completely random place where nobody knew him. Even if he didn't buy a ticket, though, the money was unlikely to last him more than a few weeks.

When they come to the foot of the bridge, the conductor informs them that they'll be at Golpark soon. Orko takes his bag back from the man and disembarks at his usual stop, but he doesn't cross the street. Instead, he ducks into the lane that skirts the Institute of Culture and comes out on Southern Avenue. A little girl, no more than seven or eight years old, fills an aluminium pot from the tubewell by the side of the road. She's wearing only a pair of tattered, filthy shorts. Her matted hair is bronzed from exposure and neglect. It is fairly obvious that she doesn't go to school. The pot looks too big for her to be able to carry, but she hoists it up to her hips and snakes an arm around it. Would this little girl be willing to trade places with Orko? Would he trade places with her? Who would choose a life on the street, if the choice were theirs to make?

Orko walks along the periphery of the lake, worrying that he's going to run into someone he knows. They will probably ask him what he is doing here at this hour, in his school uniform, and he won't have a satisfactory explanation. He ducks through a gate in the fence and cuts across the green until he comes to the narrow footpath that leads to the water's edge. He follows the path as it merges with a wider, paved road and reappears on the far side. The noise from the street is barely a murmur now, with an occasional spike from a horn.

He passes the Anderson Club, where his grandfather sometimes brought him to swim. To his left is a gate that leads to Southend Park. He remembers going that way with his grandmother, back when he still thought he was a little girl. They would go to the Buddhist temple and sit on one of the benches outside. Inside, the monks chanted somnolently as they beat the prayer drum in that slow, meditative rhythm.

He stays on the path as it curves sharply to the right. It passes beneath a canopy formed by the dense foliage of trees on either side, transforming into a magical lattice of shadows and light. His father would bring him here on winter afternoons, and would point at the trees they passed, calling out their names in Latin and in Bangla. Orko listened, wide-eyed, thinking that his father was omniscient. Now, surrounded by these trees that are older than he is, he can't remember their names in either language.

He can see water now. There are people here – a middle-aged man, in shorts and a sweaty T-shirt that is stretched over his pendulous belly; a woman in a saree, struggling to keep up with the man. In sneakers, both of them, with sparkling rivulets of sweat running down the sides of their necks. They hurry past him. Behind them is a younger man, with a large dog on a leash. Orko had always wanted a dog. A dog that walked by his side, wherever he went, and slept in his bed at night. He doesn't want one anymore. He has even stopped bringing biscuits to the old dog that lives in their enclave. He once thought that he cared for the creature. Now he's not sure if he actually did, or if he was kind to her in order to feel superior, benevolent, godlike.

He comes to a bench at the edge of the lake, made familiar by the stout gulmohur alongside it. This is the bench his father sought out every time they came here. He shrugs off his schoolbag and drops it carelessly on the bench. He sits down beside the bag and hugs it to his side, as if it were a dear friend. The bag feels damp to the touch. It hasn't been opened since he left Brishti's house. It doesn't contain the books and the homework for the classes he has today; he can't really claim that his truancy wasn't premeditated.

The banks of the lake are deserted. Even the straggling morning walkers have now gone home. His father is probably on his way to work now, as are countless men all over the city. Their wives are probably clearing away the table after their husbands' breakfasts. The children are all in school. The buses are crowded, the markets thick with retired men and older, matronly women carrying nylon shopping bags full of vegetables and fish. It's almost as if all of it is happening in another world – a world in which he does not belong.

A woman washes clothes on the far side of the lake. She probably lives in one of the shanties by the suburban railway tracks. Orko doesn't know anyone who washes their own clothes. His father washes his own underwear, and Orko does too, but that doesn't really count. The woman beats a large garment (a bed sheet? a saree?) on the steps of the ghat. He tries to imagine her day-to-day existence, but he can't get past wondering how she makes her living. There are countless people like her in this city. They live in slums and in refugee colonies. They work in factories and as lorry drivers, as cooks and as housemaids. There are so many of them that if they all had to live in cosy flats like the one in which he lived, there probably wouldn't be enough land in the city to build the flats on.

It occurs to Orko that his particular circumstances are nothing more than an accident. He could easily have been born as the woman on the far side of the lake. A sense of despair overwhelms him. He feels like a spoilt, petulant wastrel, strung out over impossibilities and wild imaginings. He wishes he could be normal, like other boys – horsing around during the lunch break, playing football with his buddies after school, never having to worry about men like Bishu. He can't imagine spending decades like this, growing old, pretending to be happy the whole time, burning with jealousy whenever he passes a girl his age on the street, and having the wind knocked out of him whenever his thoughts turn to Bishu and the room on the terrace.

At the ghat on the far side of the lake, the woman gathers her washing in a metal bucket. Two young boys appear. They loiter about, pelting each other with pebbles. After the woman leaves the ghat, the boys strip down to their underwear. One of them appears a little bigger than the other. Orko wonders if they're brothers.

The bigger boy descends the steps of the ghat until he is waist-deep in the waters of the lake. He disappears beneath the surface, then reappears. The smaller boy throws something at him. He catches, crisply, with his right hand. Orko wonders what it is, until the boy lathers up his face and his arms, and reaches to soap his back. He throws the bar of soap back to the smaller boy, who tries to catch it, but it falls to the grass. The bigger boy yells something to him. The smaller boy yells back. He walks down to the edge of the lake and jumps in. They frolic in the water.

Orko considers going over and asking to join them, but they're far away, their simple pleasures beyond Orko's reach. They probably live in a shanty by the railway line, like the woman who came before them. The bigger boy begins ascending the steps of the ghat. The smaller one follows.

Orko absent-mindedly casts a pebble into the water. It strikes the surface with a muted pop, then disappears completely, forever. Over the years, he has cast many pebbles into these waters. In billions of years, when the sun grows into a giant star and boils off the waters of this lake, everything will die. The trees, the birds, the insects. The pebbles that he has casually thrown into the lake will still be there, mute witnesses to the end of the world. No one but he knows where they are, and if someone were to find them, they wouldn't know that it was he, Orko, who cast them into the lake. It would be as if he had never existed.

Orko senses something cold and wet on the back of his hand – it's a dog, nuzzling his palm. He casts about in his schoolbag for his tiffin box. Then he remembers that he hasn't brought tiffin. He strokes the fur on the dog's neck. The dog appears pleased. Its golden-brown fur shimmers in the sunlight. Orko begins to wonder what time it is. He wishes he had worn the watch his father gave him when he passed his board examinations. It's a large wristwatch, and it sits heavy on his arm. He wore it for a few days, but every time he looked at it, it reminded him that he was growing up to be just like his father. He put it away in the drawer of his grandfather's writing bureau. He winds it every morning before leaving for school. He forgot to wind it today.

Orko's toes feel as if they've been set upon by a thousand locusts. He wiggles them inside his shoes, but he can't tell if they're actually moving. His calves feel numb. He raises the leg of his trousers and pinches himself. Nothing. He stretches his legs out in front of him. The dog, startled, takes a few steps backwards. He wonders what his classmates are doing now. Is it time for the economics class? Has anyone noticed that his seat is empty? His class teacher must have, when she called out their names from the register. Brishti. Nilanjana, maybe. Paromita, when she looked across the classroom to smirk at him. He realises that he doesn't care anymore.

In the past, when Orko imagined running away from home, his thoughts were never backed by intent; he merely wondered how he would feel to be all by himself, in a place where nobody knew him. He had never considered the real consequences of running away. He would never see his father or his aunt again. He would be friendless and alone, making a living as a waiter or a busboy. He would never again sit here, on this bench by the lake. He would probably sleep at a deserted bus stop, on sheets of old newspaper.

He begins to feel angry again. Bishu had no business being at *his* bus stop. He had no business calling out his name like that, in public, where everyone could hear him. What if he went to Orko's school and talked to his teachers, or to Brishti? Would they think he was a filthy deviant, and that he was an equal participant in the goings-on in the room on Bishu's terrace?

Orko imagines a sharp machete – the biggest one he can find. Bishu was bigger than him, and stronger than him.

He would carry it with him to the room on Bishu's terrace. When Bishu took off his pants again, he would chop off Bishu's penis. After that, he would run away. Of course, he couldn't do it right away. He would have to wait until he finished school, maybe even college. No one would give him a job if he didn't. Maybe, by the time he finished college, the anger would have gone away. Then he wouldn't have to chop off Bishu's penis after all.

He can wait. He has all the time in the world. What he can no longer bear, though, is not knowing his position on the balance of blame. He remembers the evening with his aunt, in the dimly lit Chinese restaurant. He knows she would never disown him. If he tells her everything, maybe she will tell him, again, that he is blameless.

There was a time when Orko took the school bus down this road every afternoon. This was before his aunt left for Dehradun, and when he passed the traffic signal before the cinema, his eyes would dart outwards, looking for the familiar figure of his aunt in her crisply starched saree, her horn-rimmed glasses too large for her face. He would leave his seat long before his stop, and wait by the door. When the bus began to slow down, he would climb down to the footboard, jumping off as soon as the conductor opened the door.

Sudeshna would transfer the polka-dotted umbrella to her right hand and take his hand in her left. They would walk down the short length of road, past the cinema, to his grandfather's house. She would ask him what he had done in school, and he would always omit the arithmetic, in the hope that she wouldn't ask him to recite tables again. She would find out, of course, when she went through his exercise books with the hawkish eye of an accountant.

As Orko walks past the cinema, he begins to have second thoughts about confiding in his aunt. He comes to a halt by a handcart laden with sugarcane. The man asks him if he'd like some juice. Orko shakes his head. He considers going back home. He would tiptoe up the stairs and lock himself in the flat. He wouldn't answer the doorbell. He wouldn't make any noise. He wouldn't turn on the stereo. No one would know he was there. When his father came back home, he would act as if it had been a normal day, and pretend that everything was all right.

Everything is not all right, though. He is tired of keeping it all to himself. He decides to press on, braving the scolding that he is sure his aunt is going to give him. He knows what he must do. He must tell his aunt everything. All his secrets. Every little detail. Even the bit about the pebbles he cast into the waters of the lake. Then, maybe, Bishu will have no power over him.

He has always thought of this as his grandfather's house. But his grandfather has been dead for a long time; this is now his aunt's house. He presses the doorbell, expecting to hear the familiar metallic clang, but the house is silent. A power outage, perhaps. He hesitates before sounding three sharp raps on the door panel with the palm of his hand.

The door opens almost immediately. Sudeshna looks him up and down and asks him to come in, as if she was expecting him. The fact that it's a school day and he is wearing his school uniform seems to have escaped her. Orko shuts the door behind him and follows her into the dark living room. Sudeshna is still in her nightgown, and Orko finds this strange. When he spent the night in this house as a child, Sudeshna would be bathed and dressed by the time he awoke. Sometimes he would wake early enough that her hair would still be wrapped in a light towel. Today, it seems to Orko that she hasn't been awake for too long.

As they pass through the dining room, Orko glances at the clock. It is half past eleven. Dirty bowls and dishes lie haphazardly on the dining table. Some of the bowls have the remnants of last night's dinner in them.

It's not like his aunt at all to leave dirty dishes on the table, or to still be in her nightgown at eleven-thirty in the morning. Orko can't see her face, but when she opened the door she seemed haggard, as if she were straining under a great burden.

They're on the balcony when she turns towards him. She looks embarrassed, as if she doesn't want him to see her like this. 'I was just going for my bath,' she says. 'Sit here for a while.'

'Okay,' says Orko. 'You don't look too well. Is everything all right?'

'Sit,' she says, by way of an answer. 'I won't be long.'

Orko sets his schoolbag down on the high chair that he used as a child, surprised that his aunt still has it after all these years. He sits on the chair next to it. This chair is also in his earliest memories, although the dark varnish has been replaced by white paint.

He regrets not visiting his aunt in these past few months. The truth is that Orko has been avoiding her. He knows that he has disappointed her. He can't decide if it is because he has done poorly in his examinations, or because the last time he was here he discovered that she had seen him at her dressing table. He still remembers his face as he saw it in the mirror on his aunt's dressing table – the face of a young girl, her lips smeared with maroon lipstick.

The balcony is quiet. The ceiling fan is stationary. Orko wonders how long the power has been gone, and then he remembers the candle on the dining table, standing like the steadfast tin soldier amid the detritus of last night's dinner. He begins to worry for his aunt. He wonders if she has forgotten to pay the electricity bill, like his father. Was she, too, worn out by his strangeness? Was she disappointed that, in spite of everything she has done for him, he has amounted to so little?

'It's so good to see you, Orko,' Sudeshna says as she appears in the doorway. 'It has been such a long time!'

She's draped in a saree he has seen her wear hundreds of times. The saree hangs limply from her body. Her wet hair, flecked with grey, is spread across her back. It catches the sun as she hangs a towel out to dry. She looks older than Orko remembers.

'Yes, it has been a long time,' says Orko. He feels like saying much more, to explain his long absence, but the sentences trip on themselves on the way to his lips.

'I've had a bad night,' Sudeshna says. 'The power went out just as I sat down to dinner. I didn't sleep too well.'

Orko wants to ask her if she has paid the electricity bill, but she's his aunt – she has always been in control of everything that goes on in this house. She would probably take umbrage at the suggestion that she can't keep up with her own affairs.

'I'll go and ask the neighbours if they know anything,' he says.

'My little Orko is not so little anymore,' Sudeshna says, smiling. 'Yes, you better go find out what's wrong.'

On his way out, Orko notices that the house looks more unkempt than ever. The dishes have now been cleared away, but the rancid smell of spoiling food hangs in the air. The dining chairs are all askew. There's a filthy rag on the towel rack by the washbasin. In the living room, there are old newspapers on the sofa and on the writing bureau. On the floor, between two chairs, is an empty biscuit wrapper. He makes sure his aunt isn't watching, picks it up and stuffs it into his pocket. He draws his finger across the surface of the bookshelf. It comes away dusty; the bookshelf probably hasn't been dusted in weeks. In the past few months, he has often been distraught at the state of his own room, but he has never let it get so out of hand. It wouldn't disturb him so much, he figures, if his aunt wasn't normally so fastidious. He can't imagine that she spent the whole night with no electricity without bothering to investigate the matter.

Orko feels unreasonably anxious as he stands at the gate of the neighbours' house. He has been here, as a child, with his grandfather. This would be his first visit since his grandfather's passing. He walks past the open gate. Through a window he can see the ceiling fan spinning away. He turns away, glad to have avoided having to speak to someone he doesn't really know.

'I think there's something wrong with the circuit here,' he says to his aunt. 'The neighbours have power. Maybe a blown fuse?' He feels silly saying this. His father would know what to do. He would probably have located the blown fuse and fixed it by now, without having to bother the electrician. Orko doesn't even know where to find the electrician.

'This house is a millstone around my neck,' Sudeshna laments. 'Every day brings new calamities.'

'Shall I call the electrician?' Orko asks.

'No,' says Sudeshna. 'He'll charge an arm and a leg just for showing his face. Wait here. I'll go get the neighbours' driver to come and look at it.'

Orko wonders if Sudeshna is having money problems. She doesn't have a job. His grandfather had a pension from the government, but surely that must have been discontinued after his death. It is very likely that she only has the money she earns from tutoring schoolchildren. His father once told him that she had been on track to become the headmistress of the school where she worked, but she had left it all behind and came to Calcutta to look after her father. Now she is alone in this rambling old house, helpless and, possibly, in financial straits.

The two women who worked in the household have obviously been let go. The layers of dust in the dining room, the biscuit wrapper and the unwashed dishes are testament to the fact that she couldn't keep up with it all. In spite of being so hard up, she had arranged the pujo for his wellbeing. He had attended, but he hadn't really participated. He didn't have the courage to tell her point-blank that he didn't believe it would do him any good, and he didn't have the grace to absorb the spirit of the pujo, or to appreciate how important he was to his aunt. How ungrateful he had been! How insensitive!

The sound of Sudeshna's voice breaks Orko's train of thought. 'It was the fuse. What a clever young man you are,' she says from inside the room. Orko leaves his seat by the railing and goes back into the dining room. The fluorescent light has come back on, and the fan is beginning to gather speed.

He turns off the light. 'It was just a lucky guess,' he says. 'Baba would have known right away. He probably would have been able to fix it himself.'

'How is your father?' Sudeshna asks. 'I haven't heard from either of you since the pujo.'

'I'm so sorry, mashi,' he says. The apology sounds hollow, incomplete. He stands there in silence as his aunt washes the dishes from last night's dinner. He would offer to help, but he knows his aunt will turn him down.

'I missed you,' he says. 'It's been such a long time. I thought I would come and visit you.'

He feels terrible about lying to his aunt. Of course he hasn't missed her. He isn't here to find out how she is doing. He has come here to unburden himself. As a matter of fact, on his way here, all he had thought about was absolution, of which he now feels undeserving. He is to blame for all his troubles. His aunt, on the other hand, has real problems. She is all alone. She had looked after him, and his grandfather, when they were helpless. It is his turn to look after her, and he has been derelict in his duty.

'It's been such a terrible night, and I've been so distracted that I haven't even asked you if you're hungry,' says Sudeshna, smiling at last. 'You must be. Shall I make you an omelette?'

Orko is hungry. He could do with much more than an omelette. He nods.

He follows his aunt to the kitchen, watching her every move. Her limbs seem less sure of themselves than he remembers, her manner more subdued than he knows her to be. She brings two eggs from the refrigerator. She breaks them against the edge of a mug that Orko recognises as the one in which his grandfather was served a milky porridge every morning. She beats the eggs with a fork, pausing briefly to add a dash of salt. She sets the frying pan on the stove, and breaks two matchsticks before she succeeds in lighting the flame. She measures out a spoonful of oil and, with a flick of her wrist, lets the oil fall onto the surface of the frying pan. At last, she seems in control.

Orko remembers the evening at the Chinese restaurant. He doesn't want her to feel the way she did that evening. He doesn't want to leave her distraught, straining under the weight of his secret, alone in this old house with its fickle fuses, its furniture layered in dust.

When Orko leaves his aunt's house an hour later, his secret is still with him, like a foul stench that refuses to fade away.

Thirteen

It is past noon, and the air is thick with moisture; yesterday's rain is now the perspiration on Orko's brow. He walks aimlessly, without a particular destination in mind. It doesn't seem like a very long time before he finds himself back at Golpark, across the street from the stop where he waits for his bus every afternoon. He crosses the street and walks past the bus stop, to a tea stall on the footpath. He sits down on the bench and asks for some tea.

Men pass on the footpath – some of them seem like they're in a tearing hurry; others just saunter along. Orko assigns names to them: Mr Bose, Sadhan-babu, Mintu-da. Orko has come across hundreds, maybe thousands of men like them. They aren't bad people. They're happy, successful, useful to society. They work at offices and banks, and some of them do important things. On their way home, when the creases in their trousers lose the edge, they stop at tea stalls like this to smoke their cigarettes and drink sweet tea, piping hot, from tiny earthen cups. Some of them dip biscuits in their tea – biscuits that look like butterflies.

Once, Orko saw a young woman at this tea stall. She had come with a man who was about the same age as her. There were four men, older, sitting on the bench, arguing about football. The World Cup was on at the time, and he heard the words 'Brazil' and 'Argentina' spoken fervently, as if they were the names of gods or great warriors. One of the men said, loudly enough for the woman to hear: 'Look at the lovebirds!' The others laughed. Someone commented on the clothes the woman was wearing, remarking that she looked sexy. The young couple slunk away, as if they had fallen afoul of an unwritten rule.

The memory brings with it a flash of anger. Who made these rules? Who gave those men the right to enforce these rules in that odious way? He thinks about Bishu's teachings, and their sheer absurdity leaves him incredulous. He drains the earthen cup and tosses it into the wastebasket by the bench. He leaves a two-rupee coin on the counter and walks away, towards the boulevard. The shopkeeper calls after him, reminding him to take his schoolbag. Orko slings it over his shoulder and turns away, too embarrassed to thank the man.

On the boulevard, the shopkeepers are preparing their makeshift stalls for the day ahead, setting out their wares on countertops or stringing them up on lengths of nylon cord. A man with a cloth duster polishes the glass door of the photo studio. Orko steals a glance at his reflection in the glass. Beside the photo studio is a tiny sliver of a shop that sells underwear, and past it is a jeweller's. On the signboard, below a crude illustration of the various gemstones that might be purchased there, is a declaration that Orko thinks he had seen when he passed the shop on his way back from school. In a crooked blue typeface, it says: 'Piercings done here'.

The man at the counter looks up as Orko walks through the door. He's wearing a monocle. Orko waits for the man to ask him what he wants, but the man just looks at him, sizing him up. Orko is ill at ease. On any other day he would turn around and walk out of the shop.

'I'd like my ears pierced, please,' he says, trying his best to sound as if he has given this some thought.

'Hmm,' says the man. He takes off the monocle and places it on the counter. 'Just one ear, or both?'

Some people do wear a solitary earring, usually on their left ear, but that is not what Orko wants. 'Both,' he replies.

'I'll do it for free if you buy earrings from me,' the man says.

Orko's pulse races. 'How much?' he asks, fingering the currency notes in his pocket.

'Well, let's see,' says the man. 'For fresh piercings, you want gold. Anything else will give you an infection.' He reaches below the counter and brings out a small jewellery box. 'I have just the thing for you,' he says, opening the box and laying it on the counter. In it is an assortment of tiny golden earrings.

'The studs are two hundred rupees,' he says. Then, pointing at a pair of tiny hoops like the ones Urmi used to wear to school, 'These will cost you three hundred. I don't think any of the others will suit you.'

The man is right. Orko can't imagine wearing the large hoops, or the ones set with fake gemstones.

'I'll take these,' he says, pointing at the little hoops. He removes the wad of cash from his pocket. The man watches him count out three hundred rupees, in ten- and twenty-rupee notes. Orko sets the money down on the counter, and the man puts it away in a drawer. He latches the door and draws the curtains. 'Come with me,' he says.

Orko follows the man into a well-lit antechamber. The walls are lined with shelves, most of them empty. Some are stacked with jewellery boxes, large, medium, small. In one of the shelves is a series of ornate gold necklaces in open cases.

'Sit down,' the man says, pointing at a stool beside the door. On a workbench in the corner is an assortment of tools that look like they're from an alien civilisation. Orko recognises a Bunsen burner, and a pair of tweezers lying by its side. The man fires up the burner before rummaging in a drawer for a few seconds and bringing out a well-worn leather pouch. From the pouch he removes a metal stalk, about the size of a crochet hook. From another drawer he brings out a bottle of Dettol and a wad of cottonwool. He moistens a swab of cottonwool with the antiseptic and wipes down the tip of the stalk. He uses the same swab to wipe Orko's earlobes and the tiny golden hoops. He holds the stalk over the burner until it turns blue.

'Hold still,' he says. 'It's going to hurt a little.'

Orko is as still as he can be. The man's fingers are on his earlobe now, and he feels a prick, like an exceptionally painful injection. The pain is momentary, and is followed by a sharp, burning sensation where the piercing must be. 'This one looks good,' says the man, and moves on to the other earlobe. This time it doesn't hurt as much. The man picks up an earring, and Orko winces when he loops it through the piercing.

'Can I put on the other one myself?' he asks.

'It's better that I do it,' the man says. 'You might end up inflaming the piercing. It's going to be a little tender for a few days.' When he's done, they return to the shop.

The man unlatches the door before returning to his post behind the counter. 'You shouldn't take them off for the first week or so,' he warns. 'The piercings will close up if you do.'

Out on the footpath again, Orko anxiously studies the faces of strangers, watching for signs of contempt, or of ridicule. There seem to be many more people out and about now, and they go about their business, asking to see nighties and bedcovers and haggling over prices. Nobody seems to mind, or even care, that he has broken a rule that he has always thought was inviolable.

It's not that he has never seen a man wear earrings, but those men are nothing like him. They inhabit film magazines and the covers of music albums. They have a certain swagger about them, and some of them wear carefully manicured stubble. They don't walk about in school uniforms on the footpaths of Gariahat, and they don't look like anyone ever teased them for not being masculine enough.

Orko's anxiety comes and goes in waves. He doesn't know what he will tell his father about the earrings. Going by the way things have been between them lately, it's likely that his father won't even notice. Perhaps he will reason with his teachers that everyone else in his class wears earrings. Then there are people like Kaushik and Pratik, with whom there is no reasoning. 'Fuck off' is what he's going to say to them. The woman walking in front of him whirls around, and Orko realises that he said the words aloud, loud enough for her to have heard him. He averts his eyes and steps off the footpath. He walks along the edge of the pavement until he comes to the bus stop.

Orko has been at this bus stop hundreds of times. Today there are five men and a woman waiting with him. The woman is wearing earrings, and although Orko's earrings aren't as pretty, he feels no envy. Every few moments he is tempted to touch his earlobes. He resists – he doesn't want to let on that he's a newbie.

The conductor stares at Orko's ears as he hands Orko his ticket, and Orko remembers what Brishti had said to him and stares back at the conductor. The conductor looks away, embarrassed. Orko feels triumphant, but only for a moment. It dawns on him that he lacks even the most basic skills that his friends have. He would never have known that he ought to stare back at people who stare at him. No one has taught him that he should run away if men like Bishu try to approach him, or that he should avoid being alone with boys like Kaushik.

His mother told him that he was a boy, and he ought to be brave and strong, that he would grow up to be a great man, and that he was going to rule his own little piece of the world. For as long as he has known that he's a boy, he has wished that he wasn't, and yet he doesn't know the first thing about navigating the world as a girl. Brishti was right. It is unfathomable that he wishes he was a girl. It doesn't make any sense.

When he was very young, he used to think that he wished he was a girl because boys couldn't have earrings. As he grew older, the feeling didn't go away, and he thought he felt this way because all his friends were girls, and they shared secrets among themselves that they would never share with him. Now he's wearing earrings, just like the ones Urmi had when they were seven, and Brishti is the closest friend he has ever had. They have lunch together every day; they love the same music; they're strange in ways that none of their classmates are; they spend most of their waking hours together, sharing secrets that no one else could even begin to imagine. And yet, Orko still wishes he was a girl, and he can't say why. It's like asking someone why they like roasted peanuts, or the colour blue.

A few minutes after he reaches home, Brishti rings. She asks him why he wasn't in school today, and he says he'll tell her when they meet tomorrow.

For dinner, Orko and his father go to the dingy restaurant for the third time this week. They're sharing a bowl of chow mein and a portion of chilli chicken. Orko tells his father that he's doing well in school now, and that his teachers are pleased with him. This, at least, is true. Then he starts talking about typing school, although he hasn't been there for weeks now. He says that his typing has hardly any mistakes these days, and that his speed is up to thirty words a minute. He talks about the new friends he has made there, and says that he is going to go play football with them on Saturday. His father merely nods through all of this. When they're nearing the end of their dinner, Orko falls silent. He's afraid that the more he speaks, the more lies he's going to tell his father.

'Do you intend to wear those to school?' Nandan asks, and Orko knows that he's referring to the earrings.

'Yes,' he replies.

'Are you sure you're allowed to?'

'Well, all my classmates wear earrings,' Orko says. 'Why can't I?'

His father doesn't say anything more about the earrings, and Orko wonders if it is because he sees Orko's point, or if it's because he doesn't really care.

'I hate this restaurant,' Orko says as they're leaving. 'Can we not come here again?'

'Why don't you learn how to cook, then?' his father says. 'I'm tired of spending my evenings in the kitchen.'

'Okay,' Orko says. 'I will.'

His father is a little taken aback, but he doesn't say anything.

When they get home, Orko bids his father goodnight and retires to his room. He bolts the door behind him. He doesn't brush his teeth or change into his pyjamas. He lies in the dark, eyes wide open. He brings his hands to his ears, tracing the earrings with his index fingers. The earrings are delicate; if he isn't careful, he might bend them out of shape. In the few hours that he has worn them, things have begun to seem just a little different. He feels more confident than ever. He isn't scared of Bishu, and he isn't scared of Kaushik. They seem laughably insignificant, and he can't believe that he allowed them so much power over his life. Nothing seems impossible now. He feels as if he can do exactly what he wants to, without worrying that he's being too audacious.

He falls asleep, and when he wakes it is still dark. He tries to piece together a dream he had while he slept. He was swimming in the lake; his mother was watching him from a bench on the far shore. She was wearing the saree from the photograph on the refrigerator. He swam towards her, but even as he dreamed, he knew she was unreachable.

It's a little after four in the morning. Orko silently closes the front door behind him. He descends the stairs swiftly, quietly. When he turns the key in the lock of his bicycle, the spring-loaded shaft recedes into its sleeve with a resounding clang.

He wheels the bicycle down the cobbled path, past the pale green Ambassador in the parking lot, towards the gate. He's afraid that the caretaker is going to stop him and ask where he is going at this hour, but there's no one at the gatehouse. He mounts the bicycle and pedals away swiftly. He rides out of their winding lane and onto the deserted thoroughfare. There's a mild chill in the air. The wind is in his hair, and it whistles in his ears. Before he knows it, he is cycling past the bus terminus and through the deserted market. The footpaths are strewn with yesterday's detritus – the sheets of newspaper on which the vegetable sellers squatted, with their wares spread around them on old jute sacks; bruised tomatoes that no one wanted; cabbage leaves; the tip of a carrot; the pimpled skin of jackfruit. The grocery shops are shuttered. There's a milk van, its engine idling, near the back entrance of a sweet shop. A man is asleep by his rickshaw, covered from head to toe in a dark shawl. Orko rides past, his weariness falling away as he gathers speed. The street lights recede in the rear-view mirror; the lanes zoom out, like a scene from a movie.

As he approaches the foot of the bridge, he lifts himself off his seat and squeezes every ounce of energy he has through the pedals until he is going faster than ever. He can hear himself pant, and beads of perspiration trickle down his forehead. He takes a hand off the handlebars to wipe his brow. The momentum bleeds off as he ascends the bridge, but he remains on the bicycle for as long as he can.

When it comes to a standstill, he dismounts. He walks up the slope, pushing the bicycle along by his side. At the crest, he lifts it onto the narrow footpath and props it up against the guardrail.

He knows this bridge intimately. He has crossed it on almost every day of his life. It always seemed so grand, so high, teeming with cars and buses and scooters. Now, it is deserted. In the dark, the bridge doesn't seem as high as it usually does. The lights from the suburban railway station seem closer than he remembers. For a moment, everything seems absurd – this bridge, the railway tracks below, the orange glow of the halogen lamps in the distance. He can't imagine this scene as being a part of his life. The lone headlight of an approaching train lights up the railway tracks. They shimmer, like luminous snakes beneath the surface of a dark ocean. The train passes, and the tracks are dark again.

Orko drags his bicycle off the footpath and onto the road. The stand clatters against the mudguard as the rear wheel meets the pavement. He mounts his bicycle, glancing at the receding train as it gathers speed. He pedals for all he's worth, until he himself is going as fast as a train, scything through the crisp dawn.

Past the foot of the bridge there's a sweeping turn to the left. Orko coasts, catching his breath. The moon is just a few hairs short of full. Drenched in sweat, Orko resumes pedalling, weaving through the alleys of Southend Park, rising from his seat, his calves taut with anticipation. He passes through the gate that leads to the paths around the lake. Soon he is at the ghat where the two boys had been; it seems incredible that it was only yesterday when he saw them here. He props the bicycle up against a tree by the ghat.

He strips down to his skin, leaving his clothes in a heap on the steps.

He walks gingerly to the water's edge. He is completely naked, like the girl in his mother's notebook. He curls his toes around the edge of the embankment, hesitating, for just a moment, before leaping into the dark water.

Acknowledgements

Fern Road is a story I have thought about for more than twenty years. Although it is short for a novel, it has taken me close to five years to write it. It would not exist if not for the good people who have helped me along the way, and I thank each one of you.

Nazes Afroz and Venkat Srinivasan – you were among my first readers; your words of encouragement and the corrections you made to the prose have remained with me through this journey.

Jia, Malini Bhattacharya and Avijit Kundu – you have patiently read several iterations of mangled prose, and your observations helped me arrive at an important decision about the direction of the story.

Meheli Sen – you were among the first to read the finished draft, and your comments about the end helped improve it.

Julian Welch – your edits on the final draft were invaluable.

Sampurna Chattarji – you are an inspiration. The support I have received from you and your family have kept me going when I struggled to find the energy.

Ruchira, Antara and Tara – I was able to write this story only because I live with people like you. Sorry for being such a grouchy old man (sometimes).

The good people at UWA Publishing – it was a magical moment to see the cover and the typeset pages, and I know that a lot more has gone into the production of this book.

My friends and well wishers who have enquired enthusiastically about the progress I was making – you have been patient and you have been kind. Your support has meant a lot to me.

Terri-ann White – if I believed in miracles, I would say that it was a miracle for me to have met you. Your astute observations and your unflinching criticism taught me more than I could have hoped to learn. You have been patient and generous, and you have helped me through the most difficult phase of writing this novel. Without you, *Fern Road* would be a much poorer story.